Double Mocha Blues

Joss Miller Mystery, Book 1

Tyora Moody

Tymm Publishing LLC

Double Mocha Blues
Joss Miller Mysteries, Book 1

Copyright © 2023 by Tyora Moody

Double Mocha Blues is a work of fiction. Names, characters, places and incidents either are products of the author's imagination or are used fictitiously. Any resemblance to actual persons, living or dead, events, or locales is entirely coincidental.

Published by Tymm Publishing LLC
www.tymmpublishing.com

Paperback ISBN: 978-1-961437-23-4
Ebook ISBN: 978-1-961437-10-4

Cover Design: TywebbinCreations.com
Editing: Felicia Murrell

Chapter 1

Double Delights

Urban Radio Station
Charleston, SC

DJ Nyla B: What's up, Sugar Creek! We have our very own Joss Miller on the show today. Joss, thank you for being here today.

Joss: Thank you for having me.

DJ Nyla B: Not a problem, girlfriend. Now me and you go way back. Tell our listeners about your recently launched true crime podcast. I hear it's getting a lot of attention. Why did you start it?

Joss: Sure! *The Cold Justice Podcast* dives into real stories of victims of a crime. This first season is very close to home for me. The circumstances of my grandfather's death in 1968, have never really been addressed, and I don't want people to forget what happened.

DJ Nyla B: I feel you, girl. It takes a lot of courage to delve into personal and often painful stories. Can you give our listeners a glimpse into your grandfather's case?

Joss: Absolutely. My grandfather, August Manning, was a beloved member of this community. He was a kind-hearted man who, I've been told, was one of the greatest baseball players in the South. It was his dream to play major league baseball like Jackie Robinson. His murder was never fully investigated, but many of the young men who beat him to death were from prominent families in the community.

DJ Nyla B: That's tough. It sounds like you're on a mission to seek justice for your grandfather. Can you tell us a little about what listeners can expect from the podcast?

Joss: Certainly. The podcast will take listeners on a journey through the stories of those who knew my grandfather and the impact his death had on our community. All the episodes will be available for all those folks who like to binge through a podcast. I pray it sparks some closure for my family.

DJ Nyla B: Well, Joss, your passion and dedication are truly inspiring. Thank you for joining us today. We'll be eagerly tuning in to the *Cold Justice Podcast* and supporting you.

Joss: Thank you so much for having me.

Monday, September 12, 3:30 p.m.

It's finally happening! You did it, Joss!

A sharp, burning pain zapped my hand, diffusing my burst of joy. "Ouch." My hands shook as I carefully put the carafe back on the warmer, not wanting to cause any more injury to myself. I cringed as a tiny puddle of coffee inched closer to the edge of the counter. In the excitement of hearing my morning interview on the radio, I'd actually missed pouring the coffee into the cup. Snagging a cloth from underneath the counter, I dabbed up the coffee before I ended up having to mop the floor too.

I looked down at my scorched hand but still kept an ear trained on the speakers in the corner of the ceiling. DJ Nyla B. had switched back to a smooth, head-bobbing melody. I'd known DJ Nyla B. since elementary school when she was just Nyla Masters. I knew she would continue to promote the interview and the podcast throughout her shift on the radio today.

"You should slap some aloe on that hand," a deep masculine voice advised me.

Looking across Sugar Creek Café's counter, a customer had entered without me noticing. How long had he been standing there?

Oh wow! He's new — and a total snack.

My lips curved into a grin, even though my cheeks burned, and my hand throbbed. I moved toward the register to take his order, probably looking like a grade-A klutz.

"Hey there! Sorry about that. What can I get you today?"

The man had brown eyes that oozed with worry. He sported a fade around the sides of his oval shaped face and had a tuft of curly hair on top.

"Are you okay?" he inquired.

At first, I thought I must have been staring too hard at him, but then I noticed he was focused on my injured hand. Why was he so worried? Although my hand was still stinging, it really wasn't that bad.

Hiding my pain was something I'd become quite good at over the years. "I'm all good," I said, flashing him another smile to conceal my discomfort.

"You should probably get that checked out." The man motioned toward my hand as if he wanted to examine it more closely, but thought better of it and pulled back.

I tucked my hand behind my back, keeping up the facade—smiling and holding eye contact. "No worries! Just one hazard of being a barista." It was time to get the focus off me and onto this man who'd held my attention. "Are you new here? I've never seen you in here before."

Sugar Creek was a pretty tight-knit community, and the café was a center of attraction. I felt like most residents and tourists came through these doors.

He smiled. "Just moved to Charleston. Started at CPD a few weeks ago as one of their detectives. Heard around the station that Sugar Creek Café has the best coffee in Charleston."

A detective. I'd totally pegged him for a doc.

But detective somehow upped his hotness quotient.

Calm down, Joss. You're on the clock. Keep it together.

Kind of hard to do since the man saw me spilling coffee all over me and the counter.

"Welcome to Sugar Creek Café! Our motto is 'Coffee for the Soul.'" I gestured toward the large letters written above us. "What can I whip up for you today?"

"Black coffee, please."

I smiled. My cheeks were starting to hurt. "Coming right up." As I turned, I wished the counter wasn't so open. Customers could see everything, including spilling hot coffee on yourself. Thankfully, the pain in my hand had subsided. I concentrated on reversing the poor first impression I had made.

"Here you go, Detective..."

He flashed a brilliant smile my way. "Detective Baez, Andre Baez." He looked at my apron. "And your name is Jocelyn?"

I had another apron stitched with my nickname, but that one was in the laundry. "I prefer Joss. Joss Miller."

Why did I sound like I'd just ran a marathon?

Oh my goodness, the way he was looking straight into my eyes, all I could do was grip the counter to steady myself.

"Let me know if you need something else." I turned my burning face away to look at the clock. It was almost dinner-time, two hours before closing. "We have soups, sandwiches and desserts if you want anything else."

His tongue slid along his lips before he answered. "I will be back again. Those desserts do look really good. But I have a long night ahead of me, so this will be enough for now. I will see you around, Joss Miller."

"Can't wait." He walked away, and I observed, that despite the late afternoon hour, his suit didn't have a single wrinkle.

The broad backside and what I could glimpse from under the jacket had me riveted until the door opened and shut.

I let out a long sigh, wondering what he meant by 'a long night ahead.' My hobbies included reading mysteries; police procedurals were my favorite. I sure wouldn't mind talking to him again.

Ugh, not again!

My bad habits stuck like superglue. It didn't help that I'd just reached a six-month man-drought. Every time a man stomped on my heart, I'd swear off guys until another one caught my eye.

And Detective Baez, Andre Baez, had definitely snagged my attention. I had some connections at CPD too. Hmm, I might have to do some digging.

"What was that about?"

Spinning around to find not only my boss, but also the other barista on the clock, I nearly jumped out of my apron. Both of them had amused looks on their faces, but I frowned. "Y'all didn't see all that, did you?"

With turquoise cat-framed glasses perched on her nose, my boss, Fay Everett eyed me. She wore her locs in a head wrap today, making them sit high above her head. A sly smile spread across her face, highlighting her smooth, deep chocolate complexion. "Were you flirting on the clock, Miss Miller?"

I opened my eyes wide at the accusation. "What? No." I looked down at my hand, mainly out of shame because I had been attempting to flirt. That's when I noticed a welt appearing.

Fay glanced down. "Girl, go put something on that. I can't have you around the customers looking like you forgot how to pour coffee."

I cringed at Fay's words. She didn't mean any harm by it. Since I started working here, she'd become like a big sister to me, schooling me on how to accept adulting. I'd come to her a pretty lost soul. I started as a barista two years ago. I was technically still a barista, but my boss believed in rewarding good work and promoted me to assistant manager. Today though, I felt like a total noob.

Over in the corner, I heard my coworker Hailey Ramsey, snickering. She was a tall girl with a ginger ponytail that hung down her back. We all wore caramel colored blouses with brown pants. Hailey's pale ankles showed under her pants. Her Harry Potter looking glasses gave her a wide-eyed appearance like Marcy from the Charlie Brown comics.

I gave her the eye. "You could have taken his order. You knew I was tired." I had been trying to sneak that cup of coffee for myself. I'd been working nights to get the *Cold Justice* podcast recorded and posted, and it was like a full-time job.

Hailey shook her head vigorously. "No, I would have made an even worse impression than you. You always know how to turn on the charm. That guy liked you."

With a huge grin on my face, I headed to the back where we kept supplies. Next to Fay's office and a small lounge used for employee breaks, Fay had a farm sink installed a year ago, which we all adored. I grabbed the stainless steel faucet and spread my fingers apart under cold water, reveling in the coolness.

Fay showed up at my elbow with a bottle of aloe vera gel. "Let me see your hand. I'm not trying to pay you worker's comp. Girl, I can't afford that."

I rolled my eyes. "No need to be dramatic. I should have been paying attention."

Fay grinned back at me. "Mmm, I know why you were distracted. We don't get too many folks like him walking in here. Looked like he walked in off a movie set."

"He's a detective, new to CPD."

"Oh yeah? Well, that explains why that suit fit so well across those broad shoulders."

I looked at Fay. "Aren't you and Joe still together?"

Fay had been in a relationship with Joe Phillips, a local plumber who dropped by the café at least once a week, and usually not for coffee. He always made a beeline for Fay's office. If Sugar Creek wasn't a close-knit neighborhood where everybody knew your business, our regular customers would think we had plumbing problems all the time.

She glared at me. "I can look if I want to. Men do it all the time. Plus, I'm probably too old for Mr. Detective. I'm already skirting the lines of being a cougar."

I giggled. "Joe is only three years younger than you."

"Yeah, I know, but it still messes with my head. I'm in my forties and he's still in his thirties."

"Thirty-nine. He will catch up with you next year."

My hand was feeling slightly better with the aloe.

Fay grinned, "Congratulations, by the way. I heard DJ Nyla B mention your podcast on the air. That's great that she's helping you promote."

"Thank you! And I appreciate all the support I can get."

Fay wrapped her arm around me. "I know you started the podcast for a good cause. More people need to hear about what happened to your grandfather." A gleam appeared in her eyes. "Work your magic and maybe your detective friend can help you with future podcast episodes."

I tilted my head to the side, realizing the boss lady had struck an idea. "We just met. Very awkward meeting, I might add. But you know, I could use a real detective alongside my research."

Fay nudged me in the back. "While you are recruiting help, someone needs to help me encourage Eleanor to go home. She's been typing away all day. I tell you what, if that woman didn't buy coffee and food all day, I would have to kick her out. She really uses this café like an office."

The café had lots of regulars. Most people in Sugar Creek stopped in at least once a week. Others, like Eleanor Olsen, practically lived at the café, showing up in the morning and leaving when we closed. Eleanor was an author with several published mysteries. I'd read all of her books and they were really good. I could never guess who did it. She claimed she loved the café's atmosphere and insisted being here helped with her writer's block.

I couldn't blame her. Sugar Creek Café was not trendy and sleek like the popular franchise coffeehouses. Fay's vision was to create the illusion of walking into someone's home. There were various tables, all round, some small and others wide. Each table was fitted with high-back wooden chairs. Along the walls of the café were booths with high backs for privacy. And if you really wanted to make yourself at home, Fay had a seating area in the back of the café with plush chairs and couches. That's usually where some of our residents stayed most of the day. Eleanor claimed a booth, and it was well known to Sugar Creek regulars to stay away from sitting there.

I grabbed the carafe, my mind drifting back to my earlier mishap in front of Detective Baez. Maybe he would become a regular, too. I walked from behind the counter to find Eleanor wasn't the only regular in the café.

Sammie Morrison, an older black man in his seventies, sat at one of the tables and across from him was Claude McKnight, whose long hair long was pulled back in a man bun. Claude was maybe ten years older than me, which placed him in his late-thirties. Sometimes the two men liked to play chess. I hadn't figured out the story behind their friendship, but I knew about having unique friendships.

"Hey, Sammie and Claude. I see you two slipped in while I was in the back."

Sammie tapped his fork on his plate. "Had to get some of this sweet potato pie. Fay said she just made it this morning." He held up his cup. "Oh yeah, coffee too."

I chuckled. "Everyone knows you come here for Fay's sweet potato pie more than for the coffee, Sammie."

His face crinkled around his eyes with joy. "She makes it just like my mama. I told her if Joe doesn't treat her right this time, let me know."

His table mate, Claude, broke in. "Now, Sammie, you know you're old enough to be Fay's daddy."

Sammie sucked in a breath. "Don't you know age ain't nothing but a number?"

We all laughed.

I'd heard Sammie played a mean guitar, and several other instruments. It occurred to me that I hadn't been seeing him in the café that regularly. Though he still was a tall man, he also seemed frail at times too. He used to help us coordinate Friday Night Jam, but stopped coming to them about a year ago. Sammie introduced a lot of musicians to us, both old and young.

That's why I fell in love with working here. An artist herself, Fay loved opening the café doors to all walks of life, but she had a soft spot for artisans. Every second Friday of the month, Sugar Creek Café hosted a singer, a band and often spoken word poets. Fay rotated art on the walls from local artists like Claude. Not many people knew Fay had created several of the vibrant art pieces of women featured on the café's walls.

Before I kept going, I reached out and touched Sammie's shoulder. "Thank you for letting me interview you about my grandfather. It's good to know so many people remember him."

Sammie got a faraway look in his eyes. "August was special. Many people knew him as a baseball player, but he could sing. He could have gone either way, played in a league like Jackie Robinson or sang like Sam Cooke."

I bit my lip to hold back emotion for a man I'd only seen in photos but had heard so much about in the past few years.

Claude broke the silence. "I heard the podcast episode today, Joss. Great start! Any ideas on your next couple of episodes? You got to keep it going."

"Thank you, Claude. Yeah, I have a notebook full of ideas. And, people have been emailing me stories too. It's been amazing! Oh, and everyone has been talking about the artwork you did for the podcast. It really makes it stand out among the other podcasts. I'll email you some of the feedback."

Claude grinned. "That's great. I loved creating it for you."

"You guys enjoy. Let me check on Eleanor."

Usually, Eleanor Olsen started the day with a caramel latte or, if she was being more health conscious, she ordered a green tea chai. I knew her writing was going strong when she started the day with black coffee. As I approached the booth, I could see her shoulders hunched over her laptop.

Eleanor was quite a hip dresser for her age, often sporting a tracksuit and sneakers. Today she wore a pale pink one with gray stripes down the sides of her pants. Her fuchsia cat glasses sat perched at the end of her regal nose.

"Eleanor, I'm loving your outfit and those glasses." When I wasn't in my barista uniform, I'd been described as having an eclectic style.

"That means a lot coming from you," Eleanor said, "And, you're just in time. This plot has me stuck, which means it's probably time for me to call it a day." She dropped her voice. "Quite the showstopper we had in here earlier."

I raised an eyebrow at first, not sure what she was referring too. Then I blushed, "Oh, you mean..."

She returned a raised eyebrow. "I'm an old woman, not a dead one, Joss. Did I hear he was a detective? You seemed really friendly."

"It's my job, Eleanor. Customer service. Yes, he's a detective. Detective Baez."

Eleanor picked up her freshly poured coffee and took a sip. "Mmm, I take it he's new. Probably homicide. They just had a detective retire. You know I know everyone at CPD."

I shook my head. "I bet you do, Eleanor."

"Can I get a slice of that sweet potato pie before Sammie finishes it? I know Fay wants me out of here soon."

I chuckled. "Sure thing. I'll wrap you up a slice."

I turned to head back behind the counter, and the café door flew open causing the familiar chimes to clang harshly against the door.

The girth of a large woman filled the doorway. Catching sight of me, she pointed her finger. "You! Why can't you leave things alone?"

Chapter 2

Here Comes Trouble

Monday, September 12, 4:05 p.m.

Maggie Nelson was the owner of the craft shop, Crafty Corner, next door to Sugar Creek Café. Her shop existed in the space long before Sugar Creek Café and she often made that point. Her family, the Nelsons, owned the entire block of shops at one time, but slowly let buildings go with Maggie being the last one clinging to her shop.

I placed the carafe down on a nearby table. "What are you talking about?"

The woman held her phone up in response. "Why bring the past up now?"

I saw on her phone she was displaying the *Cold Justice Podcast* artwork.

That's what this is about? The podcast.

I balled my fists at my side. "I'm not sure why this is an issue with you, Maggie."

But I knew why it was an issue.

Many people from that era recalled Maggie's father, Chuck Nelson, being especially cruel to my grandfather. In fact, I knew that Chuck and two other men were the most likely perpetrators in the beating that took my grandfather's life. Chuck Nelson lived a good life the past fifty years until he passed away from Alzheimer's a few months ago.

My grandfather's sisters were content with Chuck Nelson's death being justice, but I wanted more. The podcast idea grew out of my interest to find out more about my grandfather and what led to his death. August Manning's life was cut short by a hate crime.

Chuck Nelson had been the ringleader.

This woman had some nerve questioning me.

Maggie shook her head disapprovingly. "Do you really have to be so public about this? People around here will split into factions over this."

I frowned at her accusation. "Don't think for a second that anyone here is trying to create division. All I want is to give recognition to my grandfather's legacy that was unjustly taken away from him."

Fay strode up by my side. "Maggie, what are you doing? This is a place of business. You don't see me going next door to your shop raising all kinds of trouble, do you?"

"My family has been through enough. We don't need this kind of publicity. I just put my father in the ground."

I started to say something, but Fay beat me to the punch. "And I'm sorry for your loss, but it's no secret about your father's involvement. His reputation caused your family pain. Why don't you put the blame where it belongs?"

Behind me, I heard a chorus of agreements with Sammie's voice being the strongest. "You Nelsons are always starting trouble."

Maggie's face grew even redder. "I didn't come over here to be insulted by you."

Fay snapped back. "No, you just came over here expecting Joss to stop doing what she's doing because you can't handle the truth."

Maggie huffed. "I'm starting a petition. I will make sure you don't cause this community any more pain or trouble. From what I heard, your grandfather's death was what he deserved. He shouldn't have been messing with someone else's woman."

I lurched forward, but Fay caught me by the arm.

I shouted, "You are really going to keep spreading that lie to cover up what your father did. Chuck Nelson was jealous and felt that he should have what he wanted. You think my grandmother appreciates him taking away the love of her life because she fell in love with a Black man?"

I hated the tears that stung my eyes.

Then I heard Eleanor's voice behind us. "Maggie, leave Joss alone. You are going to get what's coming to you."

On the other side of me, I recognized Claude's voice. "You have some nerve, lady. Mind your own business."

Maggie sucked in a breath, her face seemed even redder. For a brief second, I wondered if she was going to have a heart attack. "You haven't heard the last of me," she spewed. "I will sue you for slandering my family." She quickly spun around, and I heard the chimes of the door as Maggie stormed out.

Slandering! I purposely didn't mention the Nelsons. Did the woman even listen to the podcast?

Fay touched my shoulder. "Are you okay? The audacity of that heifer."

I nodded, but a headache was forming. "I can't believe she did that! Was she for real? Chuck Nelson may be her father, but he was a cold-blooded murderer and a hateful man. He *murdered* my grandfather, and he and his buddies were never charged."

Fay rubbed my arm. "Don't worry about her. Many people are going to hear the podcast and your grandfather's legacy will be known."

Sammie said, "That woman's not right. Just like her father."

Claude added, "We can't bury history. She needs to face the facts."

I nodded. "Thank you all." I walked into the back, going straight to the restroom. I looked in the mirror, knowing my nose and cheeks had turned red. My great aunts liked to tease me. I was red boned, light complexion with the tendency to have the red undertones of my skin on full display. When I looked at my face now, I saw my biological grandmother.

August Manning's long lost love.

And the young white woman that may have indirectly gotten him killed. Now in her seventies, I'd gotten to know Louise Hopkins and I'd grown to admire the spunky woman she'd become since those days. She'd encouraged me to tell my grandfather's story, which was her love story. At the heart, that's what it was. Two people who fell in love, but society wouldn't let them be together because one had more melanin in his skin.

I smiled seeing both my Black grandfather and my White grandmother in my face. They were both a part of my identity. I licked my full lips and repositioned the bright yellow scrunchie around my thick shoulder length curls.

Someone knocked on the door.

"Joss, are you okay?"

It was Fay.

"Yeah, I'll be out in a second."

"Don't let Maggie get to you. You've done the right thing."

I nodded, knowing Fay couldn't see me. The crazy thing was Maggie wasn't the only one who had her opinion. I received just as much not so nice feedback about the podcast as I did good feedback. The world seemed to never change, just going in cycles of people hating for no good reason.

By the time I resurfaced, Hailey had taken off for an evening class at College of Charleston, which left me and Fay to close. I felt bad for disappearing, but Fay said nothing to me. She just handed me my favorite drink in the world.

"Thank you."

"Don't worry. Everything will be fine."

I leaned against the counter and savored the double mocha. Chocolate and coffee had the effect I needed. I looked around and noticed Eleanor, Sammie, and Claude had all gone. With another hour left on the clock, the café was pretty empty, which was a little unusual. Sometimes we ended up closing later because of the mad rush to get last-minute goodies from the café.

But it was probably a good thing. It had been a long day. I drained the rest of my mocha and took the trash out to the dumpster in the back.

The September air wasn't as humid and sticky, but taking the trash out was still my least favorite task. I nearly gagged when I opened the dumpster lid. Once the trash bags were tossed, I almost sprinted back to the door.

Instead, I slowed down to glance over at the craft shop. We all shared the same dumpster. Most of the time, I never really gave Maggie's shop much thought. But her outburst in the café had her on my mind. I frowned, noticing Maggie's lights were on. That was strange since she usually knocked off for the day often before the sun went down. I wasn't sure why I was concerned. The last thing I wanted was to see that woman face to face again.

Back inside the café, I scrubbed my hands and then finished stocking cups onto the counter for the next day. I could hear Fay humming in the back, and I knew she was setting out her ingredients on the small kitchen counter. Fay would arrive at five thirty in the morning, getting the café ready to open by seven o'clock. She baked items depending on the day of the week. Folks like Sammie knew to expect sweet potato pie on

Monday. Tuesdays, when the display case featured anything from baked chocolate chip cookies to chocolate truffles, were for the chocolate lovers.

Fay had to be the most talented person I knew. She'd taught art for a while to middle schoolers, but later left the profession and went to the culinary school. Her intent was to become a pastry chef. Opening Sugar Creek Café came after a bitter divorce six years ago. I admired how she invested in the café, building it up to be a favorite hangout in the community.

I wanted to be like Fay whenever I finally grew up. Despite being twenty-seven, I still had a lot of growing to do.

By the time seven o'clock came, I'd switched over the sign on the door to close. "You know you can go meet Joe. I can close up."

Fay looked at me. "Are you sure? You closed up last night for me."

I smiled. "Hey, you made me assistant manager and gave me keys. Trust me, I got this. You have plans with Joe. I'm spending the evening with my grandmother and her menagerie of cats."

Fay shook her head. "I'm sure Louise appreciates you being there. Sounds like you two are really getting to know each other, but have you thought about moving out and getting your own place?"

I shrugged. "I enjoy being there. Plus, the neighborhood is interesting, lots of good folks around there."

"I hear you. Are you finished working on the podcast for now? I need you bright and early tomorrow."

I nodded. "Yeah. All the episodes are done. Blaze helped me remix the audio and upload to the podcast platforms last week."

Fay grimaced. "How was he to work with?"

DJ Blaze was my ex-boyfriend. He was a nice guy, but he could also be intense, which was why I broke up with him. I felt like we were better as friends. I sighed. "He didn't seem to mind helping me. And I really didn't know what I was doing at first."

Fay wrinkled her nose. "You could've asked Nyla B to help."

"I thought about it, but she's so busy. Being a female DJ, she is in high-demand. Plus, I need Blaze and me to be on speaking terms. You know how much I love his grandfather Sammie. We don't need that awkwardness. Besides, it was only a few weeks in his studio. And he didn't come on to me, not one time."

Fay nodded. "Okay, I just know he sulked around the café for weeks after y'all broke up. I think Sammie finally said something to him."

I shrugged. "My mother always tells me I sure know how to pick 'em."

Fay smiled at me. "You're going to find the right guy one day. Believe me, I joke about Joe, but he's been a godsend. After my ex and I divorced, I really didn't think I would want to be in another relationship."

"I hope I can find the right guy. All my friends are getting married now. I'm kind of feeling left out."

Fay shook her finger at me. "Don't get into that comparison thing. That's dangerous for your mental health. Focus on the podcast."

I gave Fay a thumbs up. "I hear you, boss. Anyway, I released all the episodes at one time, so it's just a matter of promoting and hearing what people say." I huffed, thinking about earlier. "I guess Maggie already listened."

Fay grimaced. "Girl, don't pay that woman any attention. She knows her dad was the ringleader. It's common knowledge that being born into the wealthy, influential Nelsons, he got away with murder."

"You know, I could have spent several episodes dragging the men who beat my grandfather to death, but I figured why bother? They're all dead. I just want to make sure people know a lot still hasn't changed in over fifty years."

Fay crossed her arms. "You can say that again. I think the positive feedback will outweigh all the negative folks and the trolls." Fay cocked her head. "What about your mother? You haven't mentioned her thoughts."

I took in a deep breath.

My mother.

"She's still not happy that I reached out to find her biological mother. My great aunts don't blame Louise, but I feel like my mom still blames her for my grandfather getting killed."

Fay crossed her hands. "Your mother is probably grieving the father she's never known, just like you are for the grandfather you've connected with through all these stories about him."

"Right. You should really go. I know Joe has probably cooked you a great meal."

Fay smiled. "That man can cook. You be safe and get some sleep. Or that pretty face of yours is going to be looking like a hag in the morning."

I locked the door behind Fay. I wanted to close up because I enjoyed being in the café when it was quiet like this. The smells of coffee beans intermixed with baked goods made this place feel like home away from home.

Fay had a point. I'd been floating between homes for several years now, even living with Blaze for a few months. When I broke up with him, I needed some place to stay fast, but didn't want to return to living with my mother. So, I ended up moving in with Louise. She was lonely, and I really wanted to get to know her.

Asking Louise to talk about a time in her life that resulted in so much pain seemed wrong at first. But my grandmother had a different perspective that I'd learned to respect.

I secured the café and locked the door. The employee parking lot for the café and other shops was across the street next to a furniture store. I wasn't nervous about being out near dusk; my bright red Honda Civic sat underneath one of the bright lampposts.

I bought the car used and I'd had it for seven years. With 120,000 miles on the odometer, there were some issues I would eventually have to deal with starting with four new tires. But I needed my baby to keep rolling.

Before I could head across the street, a noise from behind had me spinning around. I had pepper spray on my key chain and reached for the spray nozzle. The lamppost in between our shops seemed to cast shadows that lurked around the building. I peered into the darkness toward the craft shop. The lights were still on.

I frowned. Maggie closed at five o'clock. Most days, her car was gone before we closed the café. I looked back at the parking lot. Maggie's blue Ford Explorer still sat parked about two cars down from mine.

Maybe she was working late stocking merchandise.

For a moment, I wondered if I should go talk to her. Wasn't that what was wrong? People rarely tried to see other people's perspective. I knew how it felt to lose your dad. When my dad passed, it changed everything in my family.

My mom.

My brother who never called to check on us.

And me. A daddy's girl.

I could see why Maggie would want to protect her father, though he didn't deserve it. He was her dad.

I shook my head.

No, I don't want to talk to her.

But something caught my eye that I knew was truly out of the ordinary.

"Trixy." I said out loud, not believing that I was seeing the plump orange cat wandering around the Crafty Corner door. I had only been next door a few times, mainly to pick up some supplies for my grandmother, who liked to knit. Maggie kept two cats in the shop. Apparently, they lived there and walked around the store like they owned the place. Trixy and his companion Midnight, a sleek black cat, never left the shop.

So why was Trixy outside?

My feet guided me over closer to the door, though my head told me I should leave.

I loved animals; my grandmother had three cats. My imagination ran wild as I thought of how upset Maggie had appeared earlier. Her face had turned so red and she wasn't the healthiest woman. Suppose she'd had a heart attack or a stroke. Against my better judgment, I walked up to the door.

Trixy, not really knowing me very well, must have sensed I was a cat person of sorts and came right up to me.

I reached down to scratch his head. "Are you okay? You shouldn't be out here."

The cat meowed in return and turned around, tail flicking as he waltzed back inside.

The door was slightly ajar. I frowned as I noticed the sign on the door still displayed open.

Why was Maggie here so late?

I hesitated for a few more seconds before pushing the door open. A chill wrapped around me as I entered. Maggie kept her shop cold, but even with the warm temperature outside, it felt almost like walking into a freezer.

There wasn't a single sound other than the whoosh of the door opening. When I stepped inside, it was creepy quiet, not comforting like the café.

I called out. "Maggie, are you alright? It's Joss from the café."

The woman's lack of response raised the hairs on my arm.

I *really shouldn't have come in here.*

Taking a deep breath, I called her name once more. This time I heard a noise. It wasn't a vocal response, but it sounded like mewing. Kind of like when one of my grandmother's cats wanted attention.

Trixy had disappeared after I stepped inside the shop, and there was no sign of Midnight. I tiptoed toward the noise, which seemed to come from the right a few aisles up. I passed by an aisle of silk flowers and other items for creating floral arrangements.

As soon as I turned the corner, I wished I hadn't.

Both Trixy and Midnight were sitting, licking their paws and washing their faces. They took turns glancing at me, their feline eyes giving me a once over.

The cats gazing at me didn't bother me. Above them were rows of doll heads of various complexions, all staring at me. But even the creepy dolls didn't grab my attention. It was the shoes sticking straight up. I recognized the yellow crocs Maggie wore earlier. Her feet were definitely in them.

I barely recognized my voice as I croaked out. "Maggie, are you alright?"

Oh no! Did she fall and have a heart attack or a stroke?

She was so livid earlier. I pulled out my phone and dialed 911.

I don't know why I didn't just stop and make the call. Instead, I kept walking toward Maggie as if a force was pulling me. Then I looked down. Startled, I jumped back, my actions causing both cats to scurry in the opposite direction.

In my confusion, I heard a voice. "911, what's your emergency?"

I was aware of my hands gripping my phone, but the pool of blood leaking from under Maggie's head had me choking on my fear.

Chapter 3

Double Trauma

Monday, September 12, 7:12 p.m.

With shaky hands, I reopened the café and walked inside, flipping on all the lights. There was no way I could go home now. Not after seeing that!

After several tries, I'd finally relayed to the dispatcher that I found a dead body next door. The 911 operator told me to wait outside. I told them I would be next door at the café. I closed the craft shop door behind me to ensure the cats didn't escape. Trixy being outside was a red flag, alerting me that something was wrong. I felt bad for the cats having to see their owner like that. I felt bad for me.

I walked behind the counter of the café and stood staring at nothing in particular. I couldn't get the image of Maggie's eyes out of my mind. Her face had been contorted into a shocked expression. Maybe she'd had a heart attack and fell, hitting her head. It didn't appear to be any life in her eyes.

Could someone have pushed her down? Maybe they bashed her over the head. That would explain the pool of blood coming from her head. I moaned. My obsession with true crime had my mind on overdrive.

I needed to slow down. And, I needed help.

I had others on speed dial, but I couldn't bring myself to call anyone but Fay. She would know what to do in this situation. I at least needed to warn her that there would be a police presence around her coffee shop.

When Fay answered, I blurted out what I saw, tears streaming down my eyes.

"Stay inside the café. I will be right there," Fay ordered me. "And, Joss. Don't let anyone inside."

Like a robot, I started a pot of coffee. Then I leaned across the counter and put my head in my hands. Images flooded my mind. I'd never seen a dead body like that. My last remembrance of death was the last time I saw my father as he laid peacefully in his casket. Maggie's face appeared as if she couldn't believe what was happening to her.

It really bothered me. In my heart, I felt she died in a bad way. I'd never really had a run in with her until a few hours ago. Even though I knew her dad was the ringleader in my grandfather's death, I didn't hold it against her.

A soft knock had me jerking upright. I could see two tall figures outside the café door.

Oh Lord! What if it was a robbery?

My breathing slowed once I realized it was Sammie and another man.

A man I knew well.

James Morrison.

Better known as DJ Blaze.

The part about Blaze that I liked was how much he supported his grandfather. Sammie had raised Blaze, so it was full circle reciprocation.

Despite Fay's warnings, I walked over to crack open the door. "Hey, guys, we're closed."

I'd only found Maggie less than fifteen minutes ago. But I glimpsed blue flashing lights entering the street. Thank goodness the police had arrived.

Sammie asked, "Are you okay?"

I waved both men inside, so we didn't draw the cops' attention. Blaze stepped inside and put his hands on my shoulder. "You look scared."

Though I shouldn't have, I found his hand comforting. Maybe because I didn't feel so alone.

Sammie inquired after he shut the café door. "What's going on, Joss?"

I swallowed. "You are going to find out soon enough. It's Maggie. I think she's dead."

"What?" Sammie blurted. "She was in here earlier bothering you."

Blaze looked at his grandfather and then back at me. "Was she? What was she saying?"

It didn't seem important now. The woman was probably dead. I batted the air in frustration and walked back toward the counter. "She didn't want the attention on her family from the podcast. Her dad in particular, of course."

Sammie continued. "She was pretty nasty to Joss."

I knew Sammie was trying to help, but I had a growing discomfort about him speaking about Maggie. I'd watched enough crime shows to know it would be really easy for the cops to be looking at me like I did something.

Since I had company, I started pouring coffee. Fay would have to take Sammie's free coffee out of my check. Blaze declined.

Fay arrived with her man Joe in tow. She gave me some serious side-eye when she saw Sammie and Blaze. "Are you alright? Have the police come to talk to you yet?"

I shook my head. "No, not yet. Hey, Joe. I'm so sorry to be a bother."

Joe waved his hand. "Not a problem at all. As soon as we heard, I told Fay we should have some presence at the coffee shop."

Fay pulled me to the side and toward her office in the back. "What made you want to go over to Maggie's?"

"Something didn't feel right. Then I saw Maggie's cat, Trixy, outside. She never lets those cats out of the shop."

"Okay, I get that. But I was wondering why you went all the way inside." Fay looked at me incredulously.

I gulped, realizing now how stupid I'd been. My mother had constantly been on me my whole life about how I just raced into things without thinking. "Honestly, I kind of wanted to talk to her about earlier. I debated going over there when I noticed the lights on, but then..."

Fay shook her head. "Joss, there's no persuading some people when they have their minds made up. You didn't touch anything did you?"

Now a different type of fear started bubbling in my stomach. "Why are you grilling me like some cop, Fay?"

Fay let out a deep sigh. "Because when the cops come for your statement, that's what they are going to ask. You finding Maggie's body is not a good thing, Joss."

I crossed my arms over my chest, feeling chilled. "Wait. You think they are going to think I did something to her?" My voice went up an octave, hysteria on the tip of my tongue. I waved my arms around. "I figured she was so mad earlier that maybe she just fell and hit her head."

Fay cocked her head to the side. "So, you think it looked like an accident?"

I shook my head. "I don't know. There was blood ..."

Fay held up her hand. "No! I don't want to know the details. You just need to tell the cops the truth. But to be on the safe side, you might need to get a lawyer."

I threw my hands in the air. "I didn't do anything. The door was already open. Her cat had escaped and... I didn't touch her ..." my voice trailed off as the argument from earlier played in my mind. "You, Sammie, Eleanor, Claude... All of you saw Maggie come over to get on my case about the podcast. What she said about my grandparents, I could have smacked her earlier. But I never would have."

Fay soothed. "Of course not. Everyone knows you have a good heart and wouldn't hurt anyone."

I protested. "But it doesn't look good, does it? Especially if someone else is responsible for how she died."

Fay sighed. "Just be prepared."

Joe showed up in the doorway, his eyes guarded. "There's a detective out front. He's looking for the person who found the body."

I looked at Fay, grimacing. A detective. That meant the death appeared suspicious enough for CPD to send someone to investigate the death.

I must have had a look on my face. Fay squeezed my hand. "You are going to be fine. Don't answer questions if you feel you want a lawyer present."

My head pounded near my temples. "I don't want to look guilty." I squeezed my trembling hands together and then tried to shake them, repelling the tension seeping into my body. I peered down at myself. I was still wearing my uniform. I should have been home by now, stripped and ready for a night with Netflix. But here I was about to talk to a homicide detective.

I returned up front and froze— rooted in place behind the counter as I locked eyes with the man I'd just met earlier today.

Detective Baez appeared frumpier than the first time we met. He cautiously eyed me as I approached.

Why in the world did it have to be him?

Monday, September 12, 7:50 p.m.

I joined Detective Baez in one of the café's booth. Though my back was to them, I could feel the weight of Fay and the others observing my talk with the detective. Fay's words rang in my ears about having a lawyer, but I felt some comfort that I wasn't alone.

Detective Baez took out a notepad and began scribbling across a blank page. "Ms. Miller, correct?"

I nodded. "You remembered."

He smiled slightly. "The coffee was good, just like I was told. Now, can you tell me what happened? How did you end up next door?"

I took a deep breath and recounted how I'd found the door to the craft shop open and the cat wandering in front. "It seemed strange that the shop was still open. Maggie usually closes up hours before we do."

"Then what did you do?"

"I called out her name. All the lights were on, so I assumed maybe she was in the back."

How wrong was I?

I could kick myself for being the one to find Maggie.

I realized Detective Baez had been staring at me closely. "Ms. Miller, are you alright?"

His luminous brown eyes were kind despite the strain around his face. He had eyes a girl like me could easily get caught staring into for hours.

Snap out of it, Joss.

I blinked. "I'm tired. I'd just closed the coffee shop after being here all day. I really should be home by now. I know my grandmother is worried."

"It's okay. We'll wrap this up in a few minutes. Did you touch anything when you entered the shop next door?"

"No...Well, I pushed the door open, but that was all. Then, I just walked around calling her name. I had a bad feeling." I squeezed my eyes shut as the image of Maggie's crumpled body lay on the linoleum floor. "Then I saw her."

Detective Baez's soothing voice broke my recollection of finding Maggie. "It's been a long day." He flipped his notebook closed. "How about you come down to the station and make a formal statement tomorrow?"

Gratefulness seeped into my body. I thought that was kind of him. But as I studied his face, it appeared I wasn't the only one who was exhausted. "Yes, I will come tomorrow. Is this your first case? I mean here in Charleston."

He shook his head. "More like my fifth. Crime is a big deal in this city. Though I will say that this one may be my most interesting case."

I raised an eyebrow. "Why do you say that?"

"Someone really didn't like the victim."

I gulped. "She was murdered?"

"Nothing was stolen, at least from the cash register. But there was definitely an altercation between the victim and her assailant."

I frowned, wondering who went to see Maggie.

Who else did she upset besides me?

Then I wondered if I should tell him about Maggie bursting into the café earlier. But then Fay's words were in my ear too.

You finding Maggie's body is not a good thing, Joss.

So maybe I should keep my mouth shut. Not knowing how to respond, I went into barista mode. "We made a fresh pot of coffee if you need some."

He stood. "Thanks for the offer. I believe I've had enough coffee for the day."

Curiosity overruled my anxiety about finding Maggie's body. "A stakeout?"

He raised his eyebrow. "Let me guess, you're a fan of crime shows."

I blushed. "Sorry, it's just that you said you drank a lot of coffee and it's been a long day." Realizing he was staring at me, my face warmed. "I should stop talking. I just need to go home and get some sleep."

"You and me both. I will see you tomorrow at the station."

When the café door closed behind him, I let out a deep breath I didn't know I was holding.

Fay came over to me. "How did it go? Do you need a lawyer?"

"I don't know," I said, feeling overwhelmed. "But he wants me to make a formal statement tomorrow at the station."

Fay eyed me. "Who knew that you two would meet again under such official circumstances?"

"Yeah, there's no need to think anything could happen there." It would be pretty awkward getting to know a guy who had to investigate you for murder.

My body shuddered. Now I was really worried. Especially since I didn't reveal my argument with Maggie earlier today. I didn't want to give Detective Baez any reason to suspect me, but I'd been in this world long enough to know that he would find out from somebody.

And when he did, that would not be good for me at all.

Chapter 4

The Morning After

COLD JUSTICE PODCAST
Episode 1: The Forbidden Love

Joss: Grandma Louise, thank you for joining me on the podcast. Can you take us back to the time when you first met August Manning? What were your initial impressions of him?

Louise: Oh, August was a remarkable man. We met at a time when the world was much less accepting of our relationship, but we fell in love kind of the first time we saw each other. He was so funny and very sweet.

Joss: It's heartbreaking to think that August was taken from us because of hatred. How did you cope with the news of his murder?

Louise: The news was devastating, Joss. It was an unimaginable loss, not only for me but for his family and the entire community. I grieved deeply for August for many years, although I often I had to do it in private. My only comfort was that we had a baby girl out in the world. Your mother. He would have been so proud of her, and you too.

Joss: Did you ever have any suspicions or insights into who might have been responsible for August's murder? Were there any clues or indications that pointed to the individuals involved?

Louise: I had my suspicions, Joss, but in those days, it was dangerous to speak openly. The people involved came from very powerful and influential families. Plus, my parents whisked me off as soon as they found out I was pregnant. I can tell you I was very angry. When I returned back home, I made sure to never concern myself with those people.

Joss: Your love story with August is an inspiration, but it's also a tragic reminder of the prejudice that existed. How did you find the strength to carry on and honor August's memory?

Louise: It wasn't easy, my dear. I found solace in the memories we shared and in knowing that our love was real and true. It has been so good to have you and your mother in my life after so much time has passed. August's sisters have been wonderful letting me into their family. I know there has been a lot of pain, but we will always remember him.

Joss: Your story and August's legacy are the focus of my podcast. I know some people may speak harshly about me doing this, but how do you feel about sharing your experiences and shining a light on the injustice that occurred?

Louise: I'm proud of you for using your platform to uncover the truth and bring attention to the past, Joss. It's through understanding our history that we can strive for a better future. Keep doing what you are doing, honey.

Joss: Thank you, Grandma.

Tuesday, September 13, 10 a.m.

When I awoke, I could smell breakfast, which was a bit unusual on a weekday morning. Louise still occasionally baked, but she stuck to her usual breakfast of toast and boiled eggs. On the weekend, we would have blueberry pancakes or strawberry drizzled French toast. My grandmother and I both shared a sweet tooth in common.

I barely had a few hours of sleep. Wired from last night's events, I spoke briefly to my grandmother before heading to my bedroom. I'd moved in with her a year ago. Funny thing, she'd been a stranger to me when I found out her now deceased son had placed her in a nursing home. She was in good health, but her son hadn't been the most scrupulous person. He wanted to sell the house and leave with the cash, but he ended up dying in the house, which I tried hard not to think about.

I'd met him a few times when I used to work at Hooters. Let's just say when I later learned the man was actually my uncle, it made me feel sick at the thought.

Louise, on occasion, talked about her son, but I knew she was grateful to be back in her home and not be alone anymore. We'd gotten to know each other and while one day I would probably want to be on my own again, as long as she didn't think I was a burden, I enjoyed being here.

My mother, on the other hand, was not too happy with me. She still wouldn't come to visit Louise. My aunts and I worked out getting her and Louise together at their house. While my mother was always furious, she was never rude to my aunts. Although, she made sure to give me a taste of her mind later.

I always responded that at some point she needed to forgive the only biological parent she had living.

I basked in the recollections of my grandfather from both Louise and my aunts. Those stories blossomed into a desire to create a podcast.

Still lying in bed, I flipped over onto my side and faced the window. The sun shined bright through the slits in the blinds; it had to be mid-morning.

I sighed. Now I wondered if the podcast had been a mistake. I didn't know which, if any, episodes Maggie listened to, but I felt I had been really fair with each interview. My goal for each episode was to remind people of August's humanity through the people who loved and knew him. While I wanted to, I didn't present a sensational podcast that concentrated on beating up the accused.

The men were dead now anyway, including Maggie's dad. And now she was dead.

That somehow felt like a cruel joke. My purpose was to bring the spotlight and justice to my grandfather. Now I felt like last night's events were going to lead away from my true intentions. Hunger motivated me to finally climb out of bed. The last thing I ate was the last of Fay's sweet potato pie. If I had arrived on time last night, I could have eaten dinner with Louise. After a quick shower and applying moisturizer to my damp hair, I headed for the stairs. Most days I did wash n' go hair styles and since I pulled my hair back with a band, I didn't mind what my curls did.

I could hear voices as my foot hit the top of the stairs.

A familiar voice made me smile.

When I entered the kitchen, both older women observed me with concern in their eyes.

Uh oh! They know what happened.

"How are you doing, Joss?" The older African American woman stood from the table and reached out to hug me. I gladly accepted her hug. Eugeena Patterson-Jones had been Louise's next-door neighbor for over thirty years. They were more than neighbors, friends who'd raised their families beside each other. I'd met Ms. Eugeena when I was trying to find Louise. We actually met in Louise's room in the nursing home.

"I'm doing as well as I can." I stepped back and glanced down at my grandmother. "I guess you both heard."

Louise scolded me. "Why didn't you tell me what happened? I knew something was wrong when you came home last night."

I always smiled when Louise referred to her home as mine.

"I was pretty shocked. I will have to head to the station this morning to give my formal statement."

Louise pulled out a chair from the kitchen table. "Have a seat and get some breakfast. Eugeena brought over our favorite breakfast biscuits. Then you can tell us all about it."

I peeked inside the large Tupperware container on the table. "These do look good. New recipe?"

Louise brought me a plate and a glass of orange juice. "They are delicious. No one can cook like Eugeena."

"Thank you." Eugeena teased. "And don't worry, these won't hurt the figure. I finally listened to Louise and started using egg whites. I added some low fat cheddar and turkey sausage so the calorie count isn't bad. I thought Amos wouldn't like them, but he gobbled them right up."

I sat down at the kitchen table. "You know I'm eating anything you cook." That was the truth. I appreciated being treated like family by Eugeena and her husband Amos. Eugeena always prepared Sunday dinner, and Amos was the fish fry king.

Leesa Patterson, Eugeena's daughter and Carmen Patterson, Eugeena's daughter-in-law happened to be my BFFs. Living next door for over thirty years, Louise was pretty much treated like just another auntie. Besides my job, the family atmosphere with the Pattersons made living in Sugar Creek that much more appealing.

I helped myself to a biscuit and bit into it. "Mmmm. This is so good! Just what I needed." Since I missed dinner last night, I didn't hesitate to grab another one. I also felt like as long as I was stuffing my face, neither of the women would pelt me with questions, which I knew were coming.

Louise and Eugeena chatted about the upcoming neighborhood watch, while my mind wondered to last night. Suddenly, I heard my name and realized my grandmother had been calling me. "Are you okay?"

Ms. Eugeena said, "She's probably still in shock. Finding a dead body like that weighs on your mind."

"How did you all know I found a body?" I asked. These two ladies both headed up the neighborhood watch. My grandmother had been the longest residing president until Eugeena took her place. There wasn't much that went by them, but I figured me finding the body would only be known by a handful of people.

But it was Sugar Creek. Gossip spread through the rumor mill like a freight train.

Eugeena explained, "I heard from my friend Rosemary Gladstone last night. She lives right across the street from Fay. Just so happens she was returning home with her granddaughter and they saw Fay rushing out of the house. I called Louise this morning, but she said you hadn't said anything about it."

Louise pouted. "Not one word. But I knew something was wrong."

I nodded. "I'm sorry. I was in panic mode and right after I called 911, I called Fay. Then I had to talk to the detective, and that freaked me out."

My grandmother peered at me. "Why did you go into the craft shop?"

I told both women how I had a feeling something wasn't right when the cat appeared outside. "I guess it was meant for me to be around after closing to find her. There's no telling when someone would have noticed and both cats would have escaped. I hope the cops took them somewhere safe."

Eugeena nodded. "I'm sure they did. I know this had to be traumatic for you, but you shouldn't have to worry about anything."

"I'm not so sure."

My grandmother leaned over and peered over her glasses. "What do you mean?"

I sighed deeply and told them how Maggie burst into the café a few hours before her death. "She was livid about the podcast and talked about starting a petition. I have no idea who else she talked to about this, but people in the café saw us arguing or rather her yelling at me."

Eugeena placed a comforting hand on my shoulder. "If you need a lawyer, I can give you the name of the one we had to get for Carmen."

I shuddered, my best friend Carmen had been in a similar predicament, almost messing up her own wedding. I remembered the sense of unease she shared with me when the cops questioned her. "Fay also mentioned the same thing. But I don't want to look guilty."

"It's not a matter of looking guilty." Eugeena explained. "It's to make sure your rights are protected. Detectives can be tricky when they're asking questions. Sometimes without meaning to, people give up too much information and their statements get turned around."

I thought about Detective Baez. I'd just met him yesterday. Though he was good-looking and we'd flirted a little yesterday, I was pretty sure he was going to do his job. I placed my head in my hands. "Y'all, when I talked to the detective last night, I didn't tell him about Maggie visiting the café earlier. You think I'm going to get in trouble for that."

Louise and Eugeena exchanged a worried look.

My grandmother patted my hand. "You know I knew Maggie most of her life. The Nelsons, as you already know, are an arrogant bunch, every single one of them. They wielded a lot of power back in the day. Still do! It's one of the reasons why Chuck Nelson was never charged with August's murder. I guess what I'm trying to say is Chuck's children were bullies and they all created a lot of enemies."

I nodded. "So what you're saying is there has to be other people with better motives than me to kill Maggie. While that sounds good, I'm probably still going to grab the cop's attention. It doesn't help that I'm promoting this podcast and as Maggie said, I was stirring the pot."

Eugeena pulled out her phone. "Chile, let me give you the number to this lawyer. I would say at any point if you feel like the interview is not going well, then stop and call him."

I gulped, feeling my anxiety building. I could only hope that the handsome detective wouldn't grill me.

Chapter 5

The Interrogation

Tuesday, September 13, 11:30 a.m.

I'd saved the number of the lawyer Eugeena recommended into my phone. The drive over to the police station wasn't long, but it still felt torturous. I pulled into a parking space but didn't cut off the engine. The temptation to pull away and leave was too great.

To give my heart a chance to slow down, I searched my smartphone for more information about Charles Barnaby. His website came right up, displaying a distinguished ebony gentleman dressed in a dark pinstripe suit with a red bow tie. His eyes appeared kind behind circular glasses. I hoped I didn't need him, but it was good to read that he specialized in criminal law.

But I wasn't a criminal!

I mean, I had been in some shenanigans in my past that made my mother cringe and yell. But those were back when I was much younger and had a lot less sense.

I walked into the police station, the familiar scent of burned coffee and old paper filled my nostrils. I couldn't help but feel a slight shiver run down my spine.

I approached the officer behind the front desk. "Morning, I'm Joss Miller and I'm here to see Detective Baez," I said with what I hoped was a smile.

He stared at me for a moment and then picked up the phone. I gauged from the one-sided exchange that he had reached the detective. He hung up and gestured for me to take a seat in the waiting area. "Detective Baez will be with you shortly, Miss Miller."

I settled into one of the uncomfortable plastic chairs, drumming my fingers nervously on the armrest. My mind raced, trying to predict what questions Detective Baez might have for me this time.

Man, I needed this to be over fast!

"Ms. Miller." I looked up to see Detective Baez approaching, his dark eyes meeting mine. There was a hint of concern in his gaze, but the professional demeanor he wore like a well-tailored suit overshadowed it. "Thanks for coming in. We have a few more questions for you."

"Of course, I'm happy to help," I replied, trying to sound more confident than I felt. I followed him down a narrow hallway, my footsteps echoing off the linoleum floors.

As we entered the small interview room, I noticed another detective seated at the table–a petite redhead who radiated an air of authority. Her penetrating eyes seemed to bore right through me. And I recognized her immediately.

Detective Sarah Wilkes.

I should've called that lawyer!

"Ms. Miller, this is Detective Wilkes," Alex introduced us, though it was hardly necessary. "She's been helping me with Maggie Nelson's case."

"Nice to see you again, Detective Wilkes." I swallowed the lump in my throat. Our last encounter hadn't been pleasant.

"Likewise, Miss Miller," she replied coolly, her eyes never leaving mine. "Please, have a seat."

Detective Baez looked at me as if he saw me in an entirely different light. "You know each other?"

I bit my lip, not sure how to answer the question. Detective Wilkes answered for me as I expected she would.

"Let's just say Miss Miller is no stranger to the police station."

I sighed and could feel my energy draining.

This was worse than I could imagine.

"Okay, let's get started," Detective Baez said, taking his place beside Wilkes. He opened up a notepad and clicked his pen.

I couldn't help but feel a wave of déjà vu wash over me. Two years had passed since my paths crossed with Wilkes, under similarly unfortunate circumstances. Back then, she'd been investigating the murder of my uncle, my grandmother's son, who'd been shot in cold blood. That was also when I discovered my biological grandmother. Detective Wilkes had eyed me with suspicion, believing I might have had a hand in the crime.

"Ms. Miller, can you tell us why you went to the craft shop last night?" Detective Baez asked, snapping me out of my reverie. His voice was gentle, but there was an underlying seriousness that reminded me of the weight of the situation.

"Of course," I replied, trying to maintain my composure. "I saw Maggie's cat outside the shop. The poor thing seemed distressed, so I wanted to check on it. The cat lives at the craft shop. Well, there are two cats..."

I was seriously rambling, so I took a breath and tried to start again. "What I'm trying to say is I saw one of her cats and I thought he might have escaped. It didn't make sense for Maggie to leave the door open like that, so I knew something was wrong."

"Interesting," murmured Detective Wilkes as she narrowed her eyes. She studied me as if she believed I was making this story up on the spot. I could practically feel her scrutinizing my every word. I fought the urge to squirm in my seat, determined to remain calm and collected. I knew I had nothing to hide, but being grilled by a detective who once considered me a murder suspect was unnerving.

"Please continue," Detective Baez urged, his pen poised above his notepad.

I nodded and kept my eyes on him. "Once I got inside the shop, I saw all the lights on and called Maggie's name. And then I found her... body." My voice cracked as I recalled the gruesome scene.

Detective Wilkes raised an eyebrow, a slight smirk tugging at the corner of her mouth. "So you're saying that your reason for entering the craft shop was... concern for a cat?"

I felt my cheeks growing warm. "Yes."

Detective Baez's eyes flicked between me and his partner, his expression carefully neutral. "Did you chat often with Maggie since you seem to know about her pets?"

I don't know why, but this question sounded dangerous to me. "My grandmother shopped at the craft store, so I learned a lot about Maggie through her."

Wilkes replied, "That makes sense. But you must have talked to her at some point."

It was becoming pretty clear where this was going. Fay's warning rang in the back of my mind.

"Am I a suspect?" The question slipped out before I could stop it. "Do I need to get a lawyer?"

Detective Wilkes opened her mouth to respond, but it was Detective Baez who answered my questions first. "Ms. Miller, we're not accusing you of anything. We just want to know what happened last night. If you're telling the truth, you have nothing to worry about."

"Right," I muttered, feeling the weight of their gazes on me.

"Have you ever had any disagreements with Maggie?" Detective Wilkes asked suddenly.

And there it was.

I knew that Maggie's rant against me a few hours before she died would come back to haunt me.

"Sure, we've disagreed on some things," I admitted cautiously.

"Anything serious?" Wilkes probed.

"Nothing that would make me want to hurt her, if that's what you're getting at," I replied defensively.

Both detectives exchanged a look, and I suddenly felt like a specimen under a microscope. They both stared at me for a few seconds that felt more like minutes.

Yesterday, Detective Baez's handsome features and intense gaze had made my heart flutter. Today, I wished I'd never laid eyes on him. Probably because I couldn't help but feel guilty for not telling him everything. My heart rate quickened, and I twisted my fingers under the table.

"It seems like you withheld information last night." Detective Wilkes said. "It's understandable because of the shock of finding Ms. Nelson's body."

Detective Wilkes's tone had changed, which surprised and scared me. Why was she suddenly sounding so nice and understanding? This had to be a trick. My first instinct was to yell, "I want a lawyer."

But then that would just make me seem guilty.

I exclaimed. "Look, Maggie was upset with me about my podcast. Let's just say most people suspected her father to be the ringleader in my grandfather's death. That happened over fifty years ago. The story has intrigued me since I learned about my biological grandparents. The podcast is centered around not forgetting who August Manning was to his family and community, his legacy. I don't know why Maggie was upset, because I've been really careful about not smearing her family's name, although I could. But I know how sensitive the topic is."

Detective Wilkes leaned forward and fixed her piercing gaze on me. "Ms. Miller," she began, "that argument you mentioned gives you motive. Avenging your grandfather's death."

Avenging his death. So Maggie was murdered.

"Are you serious?" I sputtered. "I never said we 'argued.' Maggie stormed into the café and started berating me. Besides, my podcast is about seeking justice, not exacting revenge."

Detective Wilkes crossed her arms. "Why did you conveniently leave out such a crucial detail during your initial statement?"

"Maybe because I didn't do anything to her." I said.

"Or you have something to hide," Wilkes countered.

I crossed my arms and eyed the female detective. "I understand how this must seem to you, but I'm not going to be your scapegoat. Since you found out about Maggie's tirade, then you know there were plenty of witnesses who saw Maggie tear into me. You also should know Maggie always closes up her shop hours before the café closes. My boss left me in charge of closing the café. I hardly had any time to go over and talk to Maggie, not that I even wanted to. She made her point, and I had no plans of pulling down my podcast. There was nothing else to say or do about the matter."

Detective Baez interjected, his voice calm and reasonable. "We have to consider all possibilities. And right now, you're the one with the most obvious motive."

"Because I found her?" My voice rose, and I knew if I didn't leave, hysteria wasn't far away. "So am I under arrest, then?"

"Ms. Miller, you're free to go," Detective Baez said, his voice firm yet kind.

"Really?" I asked, feeling a mix of relief and anger.

"It would be wise to not leave town," he replied, meeting my gaze with an apologetic one of his own. He certainly was playing the good cop role, while Wilkes didn't mind slipping in and out of being the bad cop.

"Of course," I muttered as I stood up from the uncomfortable metal chair they had me sitting in for what felt like hours. I couldn't wait to get out of this place.

Detective Baez opened the door. Why did his cologne tickle my nose the moment I walked past him? I wanted nothing to do with that. My face felt warm, and I needed to get out of there.

They really were trying to treat me like a suspect.

I moved toward the exit as fast as I could, but Detective Baez was behind me.

When I reached for the door handle, he stated.

"I'm sorry about what you are going through and also about your grandfather. I know that can't be easy learning about how he died."

I whirled around. "No, it's not. He was a good man whose life was cut short. I just hope you all aren't trying to do the same to me. I wasn't bothering that woman. She came at me. This is what I get for being a Good Samaritan. I wish I'd just walked to my car and left."

Detective Baez raised his hands like in surrender. "We're just doing our jobs. We have a murder to investigate."

"Yeah, no one did that fifty years ago for my grandfather. I'm sorry about what happened to Maggie, but life is really unfair, how some people get justice and others don't." I narrowed my eyes. "I hope you don't call me back in here again. I'm going to be a lot smarter and bring a lawyer."

Detective Baez raised an eyebrow and then reached into his pocket and pulled out a business card. "If you think of anything, please reach out to me. We're not the bad guys here."

"It sure felt like it."

"Okay, I'm not a bad guy," he said with a smile.

I gulped and took the business card from his hand. When my fingers brushed his, I froze for a few moments. His touch seemed to cauterize the anger I wanted to feel.

I quickly turned around and left, my chest tight with emotions. The fresh air outside the station was a welcome relief after being cooped up in that stuffy room, but it did little to clear my head.

What was that about?

I couldn't be attracted to the guy who was probably looking at me as a suspect. If Detective Wilkes pushed, I could be the prime suspect. I saw and read enough about murder cases to know that cops had to get a suspect in the first forty-eight hours.

And this was a Nelson.

The Nelsons had always been, and still held their place as, wealthy Southern royalty or something.

As I walked away from the station, my mind buzzed with questions. Who told the detective about Maggie storming into the café? Who killed Maggie, and why? I couldn't be their only suspect. Surely, Maggie got under somebody else's skin.

My grandmother visited Crafty Corner a few times, but even Louise didn't care for her too much. Maggie always seemed to have a chip on her shoulder. The kindest I'd seen the woman was when she talked to her cats.

There was one thing I knew for certain. I had to find the answers myself.

I felt bad about Maggie's death, but I would not let it override my grandfather's death. It simply wasn't fair that she and her family were still causing problems after all these years—even from their graves.

Chapter 6

Aunties' Support

COLD JUSTICE PODCAST
Episode 2: The Sisters

Joss: Aunt Ruth, Aunt Thelma, thank you both for joining me today. As August Manning's sisters, you must have shared a unique bond. Can you tell me about your relationship with him and what he meant to both of you?

Ruth: Oh, August was like a guiding light in our lives. He was not only our older brother but also our protector and confidant. We looked up to him.

Thelma: Absolutely! August was the man of our family, especially after Daddy died. He always had a kind word of advice, but he also teased us mercilessly.

Joss: <laughing> He sounds like he was a fun older brother. Did you witness the injustices he endured, and if so, how did that shape your perspective on the world?

Ruth: It was heartbreaking to see the prejudice he encountered simply because of the color of his skin. He was such a good person and so talented. When we found out what happened to him, it opened our young eyes to the harsh realities of hate.

Thelma: They wouldn't let us see him. Mama kept the casket closed. Not being able to hear his booming voice...<pauses> It was sad around our house a long time. He was sorely missed. But Mama never wanted us to forget him. She had photos of him all over the house.

Joss: I enjoy seeing photos of him at your house. <pause> You know this podcast aims to shed light on forgotten stories and seek justice for the victims. In what ways do you hope it will honor his memory?

Ruth: I believe your podcast will reignite public interest in August's case and bring attention to the flaws in the original investigation. We know the men involved are all gone, but we can ensure that August is never forgotten. And sadly, even though it was over fifty years ago, a lot hasn't changed.

Thelma: Indeed. We hope August's story will inspire others to examine their own biases and work toward a more inclusive and equal society. No one should be killed because of who they love.

Joss: I agree. Growing up, did August ever share with you his aspirations, dreams, or any personal experiences that made him particularly proud or hopeful?

Ruth: August had big dreams. He wanted to play in the major baseball league. We believe had he not been killed not only would he have excelled in sports but he had the kind of charisma where he could've been in a political office.

Thelma: That's right! He was class president for two years and people always looked to him for his leadership. He definitely would have been doing something that involved helping people.

Joss: Aunt Ruth, Aunt Thelma, reflecting on his character and the love he brought into your lives, are there any specific moments that stand out to you?

Ruth: One memory that always brings a smile to my face is when August would tell stories at the dinner table. He had a gift for captivating us with his words and quite often, it was the only time Mama would smile and even laugh. He also had this incredible ability to make everyone feel seen and loved, and that's something I'll cherish forever.

Thelma: Oh, August had a heart full of love and compassion. He had this infectious laughter that could brighten the darkest of days. I remember him always being there to protect us. We both didn't like the summer thunderstorms that rolled up in the afternoons. Mama would make us turn everything off and sit quiet in the dark. August would sit with us and even though Mama wanted us to be quiet, he would make us giggle.

Joss: I wished I'd gotten a chance to know him. I really appreciate you both sharing your memories of your brother with our podcast audience. I want people to know August Manning was a real person whose life was cruelly cut short.

Tuesday, September 13, 1:48 p.m.

As I drove away from the police station, I blinked back the tears threatening to spill down my face. I took a deep breath, trying to gather my thoughts and figure out what to do next. The one place that always brought me solace came to mind - my great aunts Ruth and Thelma's house. August's younger sisters were well into their early seventies, but just as spry as Louise. It was nice to see older people who still remained active.

I learned about August through his sisters. While they didn't live in the same childhood home, they'd saved a lot of photos and mementos throughout the years. The sisters had memorialized everything about his life in their home.

Ruth, the oldest sister, kept newspaper clippings about August's death. She fought for a long time to bring August's killers to justice. But there was only so much she could do, and lawyers were expensive for the remaining family of three women, August's mother and two sisters.

As I approached their quaint little home, I couldn't help but smile at my memories. Most holidays and many, many Sunday dinners were spent at this house.

My mother hadn't known about her biological parents until she'd turned eighteen. The first parent she'd found was August, but at the time she hadn't known about how he died. While my mother missed out on meeting her dad, she enjoyed the relationship she had with his sisters.

Before I'd barely climbed out of the car, Ruth was greeting me. She had on her gardening clothes and a straw hat. As I drew closer, she stripped off her gardening gloves and held out her arms.

"What a lovely surprise!"

She enveloped me in a tight hug that almost had my eyes stinging. Not that it was a bone-crushing hug. I just needed it after the ordeal I'd endured at the police station.

"Hi, Aunt Ruth," I said. "I hope you don't mind me dropping by unannounced."

"Of course not, honey." Aunt Ruth's warm smile faltered after she looked at my face. "What's wrong? Come in, come in. Let's get you something to eat."

I almost laughed. My aunt's way of taking care of anything that was wrong was to offer me something to eat. Seeing that I'd missed lunch, I wasn't going to argue.

As I stepped inside the cozy living room, I could feel the weight of the day lifting. The walls were adorned with family photos, and I couldn't help but linger over the pictures of my grandfather in his baseball uniform.

Aunt Thelma, who preferred to be inside, unlike her sister, looked up when we entered. I could see she'd been watching one of those judge shows on the flat screen television mounted on the wall. I could never understand why people would share their issues before a judge and a television audience.

"Is that Joss?" Aunt Thelma set aside what appeared to be some knitting and stood. "Come here, girl. We haven't seen you in a while."

A while in my aunt's estimation was more than a week. I had missed church last Sunday. And the Sunday before last so I could get the podcast uploaded to all the various platforms.

Aunt Thelma squeezed me tight.

Double hugs. Just what the doctor ordered.

Aunt Ruth said. "I'm going to fix Joss some lunch. You haven't eaten yet, right?"

I grinned. "I don't know how you know that, but no, I haven't. I missed lunch."

Aunt Thelma patted my arm. "Well, let's get her something to eat. You could use a little more meat on your bones, you know."

I wasn't so sure if I needed the extra weight. Between my aunts, my grandmother, Ms. Eugeena, and all the stuff Fay baked, I was surprised I wasn't bigger.

As I followed my aunts into the kitchen, my steps felt lighter. The women in my family weren't very tall. I was the tallest standing at barely five foot four inches. My aunts and my mother all stood at barely five feet.

"I know I asked this before," I started as I pulled out a kitchen chair and sat, "But how tall was August?"

Aunt Ruth chuckled. "You ask that question all the time. August was about five foot nine or ten, not quite six feet. That's one thing he used to tease Mama and us about. He was always calling one of us "shorty.""

Aunt Thelma opened the fridge and took out a pitcher of tea. "Daddy died when we were young, but from what I can remember, he was a tall man, too."

Aunt Ruth said, "We were also practically toddlers. Everybody was tall to us."

Aunt Thelma grabbed some glasses from the cabinet. "That's true. But when you look at pictures, Daddy did tower over Mama." She sat a glass of sweet tea in front of me. I guzzled it down, not realizing how thirsty I'd been.

Aunt Thelma eyed me. "You need some water, too. What have you eaten today?"

"I actually had a good breakfast. Ms. Eugeena brought us over some food this morning."

"Well, that's good. Louise is blessed to have a next-door neighbor that cooks." Aunt Thelma gave me a bottled water and poured some more tea in my glass.

I nodded. "Louise cooks too, but it's not as good. Plus, sometimes I think she doesn't feel comfortable around the oven."

Aunt Ruth brought over some chicken salad sandwiches she'd been making. "That's understandable. The older we get, we can't cook like we used to. Would you like some watermelon to go with your sandwich?"

My mouth was already full of a bite from the chicken salad, so I just nodded. The older women in my life had been my biggest supporters, and I was grateful.

I finished the chicken salad sandwich and tore into the slices of watermelon. "Do you remember that photo you gave me of Grandpa in his baseball uniform? I think it was one of the last photos he took."

Aunt Ruth and Aunt Thelma exchanged glances, their eyes lighting up with recognition. "Oh, of course!" Aunt Ruth exclaimed. "That's one of our favorites."

I smiled. "Well, I wanted to do something special with it. So, Claude McKnight, the artist who has all those cool portraits at the café, he's going to turn the photo into a life-size portrait."

"Really?" Aunt Thelma clapped her hands. "That sounds amazing!"

"Yep. Fay already gave me permission to hang it in the café once it's finished. I think it'll be a beautiful tribute to him, and I can't wait for you to see the result."

"That's wonderful news, Joss. But I'm guessing that's not what brings you here today." Aunt Ruth asked, pouring herself a glass of sweet tea. "I could tell something was bothering you when you got out of your car. You look stressed, honey."

I hesitated for a moment, unsure how much I should share about my encounter with the detectives. "Actually," I began slowly, "I just came from the police station. They wanted to ask me some questions."

"What?" both of my aunts screeched at the same time.

I filled them in on Maggie yelling at me about the podcast and then later finding her body in the craft shop. After I told them, they both sat in silence for a few minutes. I knew it was a lot to take in. This woman was the daughter of the man who'd played a major role in their beloved brother's death. I couldn't imagine how they felt.

Aunt Ruth's brow furrowed with concern. "But why were the police questioning you again today? You said the detective took your statement last night."

"I think they needed something more official." I said.

Aunt Thelma asked, "How official?"

I pushed my empty plate away from me and propped my elbows on the table. "They didn't say it, but I felt like a suspect. I wasn't expecting Maggie to come and vent about the podcast. I mean, it's on public record that the police questioned her dad and his partners in the crime, but then they just went home and nothing happened. So, I don't know. It could look like I did something in retaliation."

"Joss, listen to me," Aunt Thelma said. "You're doing something important here. You're shining a light on a story that's been hidden away for far too long. Your grandfather would be proud of you."

"Thank you," I whispered, feeling the tears prick at the corners of my eyes again. "That means a lot to me."

Aunt Ruth shook her head. "I'm sorry about what happened to Maggie. Truly I am. But she had no business bothering you yesterday. She should have stayed over in her craft shop and minded her business. That's just like a Nelson to get someone into trouble. Her father, Chuck Nelson, was nothing but a bully. Everyone knew it, but nobody ever did anything about it." She shook her head sadly. "Justice was never served for August, but Chuck died a slow death."

Aunt Thelma frowned. "All those Nelson kids were trouble-makers."

I raised an eyebrow. "So Maggie probably offended someone enough to want to hurt her?"

Aunt Ruth smirked. "I have no doubt. I wouldn't worry about it. The Lord will protect you. The truth will be revealed, and everything will work out as it should. The police will probably shake a lot of skeletons out of that woman's closet."

I could only hope.

Though a slow determination to find out what really happened stirred inside me. "What do you know about Maggie?"

Aunt Ruth sighed, leaning back in her chair and casting her gaze out the window as if searching for a memory. "Maggie was always... different. The oldest of the three siblings, she stood out like a sore thumb compared to her brother and sister. More quiet and odd, but when something got under her skin, other people knew about it."

I asked, "You said there were three siblings."

Aunt Ruth responded. "Yes, there was one boy. Maggie's brother, Rick Nelson. He's just as boisterous as his father, but with a little more charm. He owns that car dealership in town. You can't miss his commercials. You know, their youngest sister got put in jail two years ago for that social security scam she tried to pull. I think she's still going to be in there a while longer."

I nodded. "Sometimes I wish I'd never walked into that craft shop last night."

Aunt Ruth sobered. "I'm sorry, honey. It's almost like all your hard work to share August's story is being overshadowed by a *Nelson*."

"Joss, you already know the Nelsons were a hateful bunch," Aunt Thelma warned, her tone suddenly serious. "Just be careful."

"Careful about what?" A voice behind me demanded. "Does this have something to do with that podcast of yours?"

I closed my eyes.

Oh no!

I turned around to find my mother, Clarice Miller, standing in the kitchen doorway.

She wasn't looking too happy.

Tuesday, September 13, 3:12 p.m.

My mother wasn't a fan of my podcast. She didn't mind me trying out new things, but her biological dad being the subject of my podcast didn't sit well with her. My mother also didn't like that I'd grown close to *her* biological mother.

When my mother realized she'd been adopted, she set out to find both parents. Aunt Ruth and Aunt Thelma immediately embraced her. But unbeknownst to Louise, her then husband encountered my mom first. And for whatever reason, the man made sure Louise never knew my mother had tried to contact her. So for years, my mom felt like Louise had rejected her.

Yet again.

The first time as a baby, and later as an adult.

Since then, they'd had a few talks with each other and while my mother was cordial, she'd never completely warmed up to Louise.

There was the other matter of knowing about how she was conceived. My mother and I both had gone to therapy, separately and together. A mixed raced woman who identified strongly with her African American heritage, the murder of the father she'd never met hung over her like a dark cloud.

Before I could get out one word, Clarice stepped into the kitchen. "Bringing up the past and airing all our dirty laundry for the world to hear," her voice dripped with disdain. "How do you know your grandfather would've wanted any of this?"

Aunt Ruth came to my aid. "Clarice, dear. Joss is only trying to share the injustice of your father's death. It's important for the world to know."

"Important?" Mom scoffed, crossing her arms over her chest. "All she's doing is stirring up trouble where it doesn't belong."

Why was my mother sounding like Maggie Nelson?

"Mom, please," I pleaded. "I know you don't understand why I'm doing this, but I need your support. Sure, I've gotten some negative feedback, but I have received far more positive feedback."

She stared at me for a long moment; her gaze searching my face. "So answer my question. What is it you have to be careful about?"

I sighed, dreading sharing last night's events. Again. "You may want to sit down for this. And please don't say I told you so."

My mother's contrite face turned to concern. "Okay." She sat down and, from the way she crossed her arms, I knew she was bracing herself for what I was about to say.

I explained about Maggie's outburst, finding her body, and finished with the police station visit.

My mother said nothing for a few minutes, which kind of scared me. I could feel another explosion of emotions, but that's not what she did.

Her eyes filled with a sadness that made me want to reach out and hug her, but I knew I couldn't. "Sometimes, Joss," she said, "the past is better left alone."

I folded my arms across my torso and hugged myself. My mother didn't inherit the affection gene that my aunts possessed. And after experiencing firsthand my grandmother's warmth and hearing about my grandfather's charm, I felt sorry for my mother. I often wondered if she would have turned out differently if she had been raised by her biological parents.

Without another word, my mother stood.

Aunt Ruth held up her hand. "Wait, Clarice. There's no need to be upset with the child."

Aunt Thelma nodded. "She's doing a good thing."

My mother shook her head, not wanting to hear any of it. She left as quickly as she came murmuring goodbyes to my great aunts.

She didn't even bother to give me her usual side-eye.

She wouldn't look at me at all. And somehow, that stung even worse.

Chapter 7

Double Trouble

Tuesday, September 13, 5:30 p.m.

My aunties tried to console me after my mother left, and I appreciated their efforts. But between this morning's interrogation and my mother's obvious disappointment in me, I was done. I probably would have curled into the fetal position right there on the floor. But each aunt grabbed one of my hands and insisted on praying over me. I never left their home without a covering of prayer.

My daddy was my rock before he died. In fact, he was a solid, dependable source of stability for my entire immediate family. My mother never seemed to recover from his death and we didn't hear from my older brother much. With that one missing puzzle piece, none of us were whole.

I kept trying to fill my holes with men that never measured up to my dad.

It wasn't until I started hanging around my aunts, my biological grandmother, and Ms. Eugeena's family that I'd felt grounded. I even started attending church, which had never really been a high priority in our household when I was growing up. I still struggled to pray, but when I did, it changed my mindset.

As I climbed into my car, all I could muster was, *Help me, Lord.* I was too overwhelmed to say much else.

I couldn't even start my car. I knew I better head out or one or both of my aunts would wonder why I still was in the driveway. I'd said goodbye to them almost ten minutes ago, but my emotions were warring inside like they hadn't done in a while.

My mother had that effect on me.

The sound of my phone ringing pulled me from my thoughts. For an instant, I thought it was one of my aunts. When I peered at the display, I recognized a familiar face and name. Leesa Patterson. We'd only become friends in the past two years after my longtime best friend, Carmen Alpine, married Leesa's brother.

I couldn't help but smile as I swiped to answer. Leesa and I often joked that we'd become the sisters we never had. Leesa grew up with two older brothers compared to my one male sibling.

"Hey, Leesa," I greeted her and finally started the engine.

"Hey, girl! Are you busy tonight?"

"Not really. Do you want me to babysit the kids?" Leesa had a seven-year-old and a two-year-old. I'd gladly accept hanging out with her sweet kids.

Leesa chuckled. "I hope you know how much I appreciate you, but no babysitting tonight. I was wondering if you wanted to come over for dinner?"

"Sure!" I replied. I definitely was not ready to head home after everything that had happened. "I'm leaving my aunt's house so I can come over in about fifteen minutes."

"Sounds good." Leesa said. "See you then."

As I drove to Leesa's, my mind wandered to her recent engagement with Chris Black. Leesa seemed so happy, and I knew it was something she'd prayed about for a long time. Carmen had gotten married a year ago and was now working on having a baby. I felt a twinge of envy, not for the first time, that my two besties were moving on with their life. As much as I loved working at the café, and loved my podcast and my family, I longed for that kind of companionship, too.

I pulled in behind Leesa's minivan, feeling a little lift in my spirits. Leesa must have seen me on her house camera. Everyone had those cameras on their front doors these days. I'd barely knocked on the door before it opened.

"Come on in." Leesa practically bounced up and down like her daughter, Kisha, would do. She did that a lot these days.

I stepped inside, not able to contain my smile. "I appreciate you inviting me over. It's been a rough day."

"Of course." After she closed the door, she eyed me with a raised eyebrow. "You look like you could use a hug," Leesa said, opening her arms wide.

I gratefully accepted. Having folks around who weren't stingy with hugs was a good thing. "Thanks, Leesa." I said, pulling back. I sniffed, detecting the aroma of tomatoes and garlic. "It smells good in here."

"Have a seat. I'll be finished soon. I want to hear all about what's bothering you."

I was no stranger to Leesa's house. Her home had an open floor plan, so I could see her in the kitchen as I plopped down on her couch. I couldn't help but notice neither of the children answered the door with her. "Where's Kisha and Tyric?"

"They're with Mama tonight," she explained.

The kids at their grandmother's on a weeknight struck me as odd, but I knew Leesa and Chris had to make the most of their rare moments alone together before they got married and moved in full-time. That made me wonder. "Are you sure you don't want this time to spend with Chris?"

"Actually, he will be here soon." Leesa took the lid off the largest pot on the stove and the tantalizing aroma of garlic and tomato sauce filled my nose. It didn't escape me that people had been feeding me all day. Not being much of a cook myself, that wasn't a bad thing. It was impossible for me to go hungry. But my waistline would pay the price with all this comfort food.

"I wanted to catch up with you." Leesa replaced the lid back onto the pot and turned to face me, her hands on her hips. "Mama mentioned you found Maggie Nelson last night. Why didn't you call me? Tell me everything."

It did not surprise me that Ms. Eugeena had mentioned last night's mishap to Leesa. The mother and daughter talked every day. Leesa told me it hadn't always been that way with her mother. It gave me hope that maybe one day I could have a conversation with my mother and it wouldn't end in an argument.

For the next few minutes, Leesa listened intently, her eyes widening as I described Maggie's confrontation at the café and then later finding her body. By the time I got around to my morning adventure at the police station, Leesa had grown furious.

She shook her head as if she could hardly absorb the events in my life over the past twenty-four hours. "They really called you in to question you. You're not a suspect."

I shrugged. "I hope not. If I become the prime suspect, my mom would really want to disown me. She didn't want me to start the podcast in the first place." I sighed and slouched down further on the couch. "I just had a run in with her when I stopped by my aunts' house."

"Oh no! Girl, you have had quite the day." Leesa came around and sat on the couch next to me. "Joss, you can't let your mother get you down. You're doing something important by sharing with the world what happened to your grandfather. I'm sure there are tons of stories that have been buried about other people who were wrongly mistreated."

"Or lost their lives," I murmured. "I just... wish things were different, you know. And I had that run-in with Detective Wilkes this morning. It was one thing having to deal with the new detective, but she really had me on my toes. I wouldn't be surprised if she didn't try to pin Maggie's murder on me. In her eyes, I had a motive."

Leesa shook her head. "But the people who were involved in your grandfather's murder are all dead. In some ways, they got their karma. Why would you go after one of their adult children? Don't nobody have time for revenge."

I started cackling. "You're right about that."

Revenge was the last thing on my mind.

Just then, the front door creaked open, and in walked Chris Black, Leesa's fiancé.

Leesa jumped off the couch. "Wow, you're early."

"Hey, babe," Chris greeted Leesa with a quick kiss before looking over at me. "Hey, Joss. Glad you could make it."

I started to thank him, but then I caught sight of the person who'd entered the house behind Chris.

Why was Detective Andre Baez here?

He was the last person I expected to see this evening.

Tuesday, September 13, 6:14 p.m.

I rose from the couch, feeling a sudden urge to bolt from the room. "Leesa, maybe I should go."

Detective Baez stepped backward like he was ready to do the same. His wide eyes probably resembled mine. "Sorry. Chris invited me over for dinner." He looked at Chris with an inquisitive look. "You thought it would be nice to get to know each other better?"

Know each other better.

I glanced over at Leesa, who was looking everywhere except me. No wonder she was so enthusiastic about inviting me over. Too bad she hadn't known about my run-ins with Detective Baez. The first time I saw him at the café yesterday was pretty pleasant, but unfortunately our meetups had gone downhill since then.

Chris held up his hands. "Hey, Andre hit the ground running since he arrived in Charleston a few months ago. He hasn't been able to get out and meet people." He looked at Andre. "Joss is a great person for you to meet."

I practically croaked. "We already met. Detective Baez was officially introduced to Sugar Creek Café yesterday." I turned my attention to the detective.

Now, I wasn't embarrassed anymore, but some emotions from earlier today stirred. "And, he and Detective Wilkes had the pleasure of my company at the police station this morning."

The room went silent. I knew my face had probably turned red because it felt on fire. Really, I could have just melted into the floor. This was the last thing I needed today.

"I can come back another time." Detective Baez turned toward the door.

"No way." Chris stated. "It took too long for you to accept the invitation. I have a feeling I know what this morning was about, but it's after hours. I know Leesa poured her heart into this meal."

Chris looked over at Leesa. My friend and her fiancé had some kind of conversation going on between them with their eyes. Next thing I knew, Leesa grabbed my arm and pulled me toward the kitchen. "Why don't you guys take it easy for a minute? Joss and I will get the table set up."

I looked at her like she'd lost her mind, but what could I do? I knew Leesa and Chris meant well. As we entered her kitchen, I felt like I could feel Detective Baez's eyes on my back.

Leesa lowered her voice. "It wouldn't hurt to show the new detective that you're no killer. Just a nice woman who is also fun to be around. You can handle this."

I hissed. "Really? You want me to have a friendly dinner with the guy who interrogated me like I was a suspect earlier today?"

Leesa gave me the eye. "He can't possibly think you did anything. It just so happens you found her. That's normal for the police to take your statement and question you."

I sighed. "What do you need me to do?"

I don't know how, but the four of us settled around Leesa's small dining room table, our plates brimming with steaming spaghetti. At first I was kind of self-conscious sitting across from Detective Baez, but one thing about eating, it gave me something to do besides running my mouth. I wasn't one of those chicks who ate like a bird, so I swirled my spaghetti around my fork and enjoyed my meal.

At least as best as I could with the fine specimen sitting in front of me. I may have still been peeved about this morning, but my flesh could not care less. After a long day at work, Detective Baez hardly looked affected.

Thankfully, Leesa and Chris did most of the talking about their wedding plans for next summer. I glanced over at Leesa's ring, delighted that she'd finally gotten her prayers answered. Chris was indeed a catch, but he would be blessed to have my feisty friend as a wife.

I looked across and almost dropped my fork when I caught Detective Baez staring at me. I really would have preferred if I wasn't attracted to him. Though I had to admit, even though the interrogation made me uncomfortable, he played the good cop well.

I flicked my gaze away from the detective. "Leesa, this is great," I said.

"Thank you, Joss. Hey, you know my mom is throwing a party for her aunt Esther this coming Saturday. Will you be able to make it? You can invite your family, too."

I smiled. "I'm sure Aunt Ruth and Aunt Thelma would love to celebrate with their old teacher. I'll check with them."

"Are those your grandfather's sisters?"

I looked back at Detective Baez, surprised he knew that. "Yes."

He appeared shy all of a sudden. "I'm listening to your podcast, and the episode I just finished was with your aunts. I think it's great what you're doing."

"Thank you," I replied, genuinely touched by his words. "That means a lot to me."

Chris piped up. "We were able to help Joss find the deputy who was called to the scene. He's in his eighties now, but he had a pretty compelling story. That episode is later in the podcast, right?"

I nodded. "Yes, Officer John Lyons is episode five. Everyone really poured their heart out answering the questions. It's been a special project."

Leesa added. "So, are you going to do more seasons of the podcast? You're really good at being a host. You make your guests feel so comfortable."

"I would love to record other seasons. I started with my grandfather's case because I'd been researching it for so long."

"Awesome." Leesa cooed. "Andre, didn't you work cold cases at your previous job?"

I raised my eyebrow at the way Leesa tried engaging the detective and me into conversation.

Girl thought she was slick.

Detective Baez stuttered a response. "Um, yeah. I worked alongside a veteran detective. It's hard work trying to find clues when cases have aged. But we had a few successes, especially with DNA."

"How exciting." Leesa gushed. "Maybe you can help Joss out with her future podcasts."

Our eyes met across the table, and I forgot all about the interrogation. Instead, I grinned like an idiot. "That would be pretty cool."

Detective Baez smiled back. "I will help where I can."

I wasn't sure if that was a peace offering, but the tension that had still been clinging to me vanished. The podcast had been a dream come true, but to take it to the next level with other cold cases would be awesome.

As long as I could get past all this mess from Maggie's death.

The conversation moved back to Leesa and Chris talking about a field trip Kisha had coming up next week. While they chatted, I couldn't help but steal glances at Detective Baez.

Andre. His name fitted him.

His eyes met mine more than once, and I caught a hint of amusement in them. We were both victims of our friends' matchmaking schemes, but so far, neither one of us had melted under the awkwardness.

Besides, I couldn't blame Leesa and Chris. They were both young and in love. Leesa had heard me pine over my many relationship failures.

Too bad things wouldn't work out with Andre, either.

I mean, nothing had changed.

I found Maggie's body and was therefore a possible suspect. It didn't help that Detective Wilkes thought I purposely left some things out when I talked to Detective Baez the night of the murder. I was sure that didn't help me in his eyes either.

When dinner was over, I helped Leesa clean up the kitchen while Chris and Andre retreated outside on the patio. As I rinsed off the last plate, I turned to Leesa. "Thanks for inviting me tonight. I really needed this."

"You know you're always welcome here." She elbowed me softly. "And I'm sorry. I didn't know Andre had questioned you earlier. If I had known..."

I gave her the side eye. "So, you are admitting it. You and Chris were trying to do some matchmaking?"

Leesa protested. "No! We just wanted to introduce Andre to other things besides the job. The man is always working. Seriously, he needs to get from around Detective Wilkes. You know how intense she is, and the woman doesn't seem to have a life. I'm so glad Chris isn't her partner anymore."

"Didn't Chris get assigned to her as a partner when he started in the department?"

Leesa nodded. "Apparently, she's not really good at being a partner. But she's good at her job, good at training newer detectives, so the police chief always pairs her with rookies. Chris said he learned a lot from her."

"Well, she certainly plays the bad cop well. I just hope I don't have to run into her again."

We'd put away the dishes and Leesa had packed up some takeout containers by the time Chris and Andre returned from outside. I wondered what they were talking about. Since it was football season, I assumed sports, which wasn't my thing.

Or, could they have been talking about me and how Detective Baez had interrogated me earlier today?

Whatever they'd discussed, it was none of my business.

It had been a long day, and I was looking forward to returning to the café tomorrow. I dreaded walking by the craft shop, but I missed being behind the counter, mixing up coffee blends and talking to our customers and the regulars.

The cool evening air brushed against my cheeks as I stepped out of Leesa and Chris's home. Detective Baez followed closely behind me, his footsteps echoing on the pavement.

"Joss, wait," he called out softly, causing me to pause and turn toward him. He hesitated for a moment before speaking again. "I just wanted you to know that despite your feelings about Detective Wilkes, she has the best close rate in the department. And her father was a former detective."

I raised an eyebrow, unsure of how to respond. Did he expect me to suddenly change my opinion of her? I knew the woman was good, but I didn't want to be under her radar.

I filled the hesitation in my response with a deep breath. And then I tried again. "Detective Baez."

"Andre." He insisted. "I'm not on the job right now. You can call me Andre."

I bit my lip before saying his name. It almost felt wrong to say. "Andre."

We stood under outdoor flood lamps that covered Leesa's driveway, but I doubted it was the light that made it seem like Andre was beaming at me.

I continued. "I know you both were just doing your job. But I have to be honest... I don't trust Detective Wilkes. She was pretty hard on me a few years ago during another police matter."

Andre's expression softened, and he nodded sympathetically. "Wilkes filled me in on that. Look, I understand. I'm here to help find the truth, too. No one is going to railroad anyone. We will catch the killer."

For a moment, our eyes locked, and I felt a flutter in my chest. My instincts warned me to be careful—after all, he was a detective. I couldn't afford to let my guard down completely.

But I couldn't deny the attraction I'd felt for him since the moment he walked into Sugar Creek Café.

"Maybe you could help save me from being pulled in as a suspect," I joked half-heartedly, trying to lighten the mood.

He chuckled, his dark eyes twinkling with amusement. "I'll do what I can, Joss. Just promise me you'll stay out of trouble."

"I'll try my best," I assured him, smiling back at him.

As we said our goodbyes, I couldn't help but wish we'd met under different circumstances.

Chapter 8

Back to Normal. Maybe?

Wednesday, September 14, 9:00 a.m.

Heading inside Sugar Creek Café, I couldn't help but notice the closed craft shop. Various teddy bears, dolls, and flowers laid in the shop's front, a grim reminder of recent events. It was strange how the café and the craft shop shared a wall, yet we never really felt like neighbors. Maggie had her own loyal customers who loved her quirky little shop, just like our café had its regulars.

I swung open the café doors, and the familiar scent of freshly brewed coffee and sweet pastries greeted me. A warm, cozy atmosphere beckoned me inside, and I felt a twinge of relief to be back within these walls after my time off. My co-worker and also pal, Briana Jones, worked today.

"Hey, girl!" Briana said in a singsong tone. Anyone else who did that would annoy, but Briana could actually sing. Like me, we both had pretty eclectic styles that probably wouldn't have gone over very well at other establishments. Briana wore burgundy box braids down her back. I wasn't too crazy about makeup, but Briana always showed up with eyelashes and her face beat, ready to go.

I'd had braids over the summer so I could survive the humidity, and I kind of missed them. Today, my hair was swept up into one of my go to favorites, a curly puff.

I stepped through the swinging half door behind the counter. "Hey yourself. How are things going in here?" I raised an eyebrow and glanced around. I had expected to see more of a breakfast crowd. Our regulars, like Eleanor and Sammie, weren't even in their usual spots. "Where did all the got-to-have-my-morning coffee folks go?"

Briana sighed. "It's been slow." She turned her head, checking behind her. She stepped closer to me and lowered her voice. "The whole time I worked yesterday, people kept coming in here asking us about *that mess* next door. Like we knew what was going on. It probably doesn't help that they have all that yellow tape around the shop door." Briana tilted her head. "I heard the bookstore owner on the other side saying it wasn't looking good for business."

My heart fell. This was not what Fay or the other small business owners on this street needed. "That's not good."

Briana shook her head, but stepped back as our boss returned from the back of the café.

"Joss, you made it in today." Fay adjusted her turquoise cat-framed glasses and looked me up and down like she was accessing my state of being. "Are you sure you should be in today?"

I forced a smile and shrugged. "Yeah, I'm fine. I just want to get back to work. Plus, you were down one yesterday. There's no need for y'all to take on the extra work when I'm standing upright." I cringed. "Did I just say that out loud? I hope that didn't sound crass."

Fay waved at me. "Of course not. Depending on what really happened next door, you should praise the Lord that you are alive. I'm still a little salty with you for going into the shop." She touched my shoulder. "Look, if you think you need more time, let me know, alright? No one gets over seeing a dead body like that."

Fay was right. No one knew I wasn't sleeping too well. The Nelsons had already done a number on my family in the past. I wasn't about to let Maggie's death take me down any further.

"I'll be okay. I really need to get back to my normal routine." I headed to my locker in the back and slipped my apron over my head, securing it around my waist. I needed to focus on something other than the horrific scene I'd witnessed next door. I really hoped the detectives didn't bother me anymore about the whole situation.

I closed my locker and headed to the front where Briana and Fay were talking. They both looked at me.

I immediately touched my hair. "What's wrong? Is my hair looking crazy? Is there something on my face?"

They started laughing.

I raised both arms, truly puzzled.

Briana shook her head. "Yeah, she's fine. She's acting like Joss."

I gave them the side eye. "Yes, I'm me. Despite everything that's going on. I told y'all, I'm fine." I stepped up to the counter and grabbed a dishrag and spray bottle. Since customers were sparse, I'd do what I enjoyed doing best.

Cleaning the tables.

Before I left from around the counter, I asked, "Hey, we're still going to do the Friday Night Jam this week, right?"

The second Friday of the month, Fay opened the stage up in the back of the café for musicians, singers, spoken word artists—anyone who wanted to share their talents. It was the thing I loved that set Sugar Creek Café apart from the big chain coffee stores.

Briana cooed. "I hope so. I'm so ready. I have some new cover songs I've been trying out."

I grinned. "Girl, you are a crowd favorite. The Beyonce of Sugar Creek."

We gave each other a high five.

Fay shook her head, a frown plastered across her face. "No, no. I'm not sure if it's a good idea with all the attention next door."

Briana and I started protesting.

Briana exclaimed. "What? Come on, so many people look forward to Friday Night Jam."

I chimed in. "It might be a good idea to get people together." I didn't want to say anything since Briana seemed hush-hush about it earlier, but the café seemed eerily quiet.

Fay only kept three employees. Having worked at the café the longest, I recommended Briana a year ago. In the third slot, Fay always seemed to keep a college student. Hailey started working during her spring semester and stayed on during the summer. I knew she planned on graduating in December.

We all loved working here. Briana and I were in the same boat. We hadn't been too good at exploring career opportunities and had stumbled around most of our twenties. Sure, maybe no one stayed a barista their whole life, but I wanted to see how the podcasting venture would go, and I knew Briana still had hopes of getting her music noticed more.

Fay sighed. "Let me think about it. It would help if the cops were closer to finding out who did this."

"Just as long as they aren't planning on pinning it on me."

Briana sucked in a breath. "The cops can't think you had anything to do with Maggie's death."

I shrugged. "I know, but her dad was the ringleader in my grandfather's murder, so it appears as if I have motive."

Fay rubbed her hands up and down her arm. "You did contact a lawyer, right? I pray this doesn't go sideways on you, but you need to be prepared."

"I'll be prepared. Ms. Eugeena gave me the contact information for a lawyer."

I also hoped Detective Baez and Detective Wilkes would turn their attention away from me. While I joked with him about that last night, it really wasn't a laughing matter.

Wednesday, September 14, 11:40 a.m.

As the morning progressed, the customers picked up, but it still felt like a smaller than usual crowd. I was pleased to see one of our regulars, Eleanor, had slipped in to occupy her usual booth. With it nearing the lunch hour, I hoped to see a few others like Sammie and Claude.

The familiar door chimes brought a smile to my face. It was good to see people ignoring the yellow tape next door and making their way into the café.

A woman wearing a very sharp aqua blue jumpsuit stepped in. Even though it was September, it was Charleston weather, so the off-the-shoulder look didn't appear out of place. It was the type of outfit I would have worn. The woman removed her large designer frames to display piercing green eyes.

Something about her looked familiar, but I couldn't be sure if she'd been in here before. I was pretty good at faces. Names, not so much. But once I saw a person's face, I remembered them.

Fay and I talked often about the café's customers. There were residents, folks who were in the café everyday like Eleanor, Sammie and Claude. Then there were supporters. Supporters visited the café, not every day, but more than once a week. Other customers were new, like Detective Baez when he came in on Monday. New customers eventually became supporters or were just tourists passing through Charleston.

"Hey, can I help you?" I asked.

The woman smiled, showing off teeth that had to have seen braces at one time. I knew about that. My dad made sure my brother and I both were fitted with braces during our preteen years, which made those years not my best years for taking photos.

"Can I get a large cappuccino, please?" The woman stared at me intently, like she was trying to figure out my identity. That wasn't hard as she glanced down at my name stitched onto my apron.

"Sure thing." I replied. I tapped her order on the screen.

"What's your name?"

"Renee."

"Okay, Renee. You can pick up your cappuccino at the other end of the counter in a few minutes."

The woman took one last look at me and then nodded. I wanted to ask her if we knew each other. But the door had chimed several times, and there was a line behind her.

Earlier, I'd been trying to convince Fay and Briana that I was fine. I'd been praying most of the morning and finding that my mind had become more at ease.

I soon lost myself in the comforting routine of taking orders. Briana took care of drinks, while Fay fulfilled lunch and bakery orders. The three of us stayed pretty busy with the steady hum of conversation filling the café. It was easy to forget, for a little while at least, about finding Maggie's body next door.

By mid-morning, the crowd subsided, and I busied myself wiping tables. Occasionally my mind would wander, but now with no one placing orders, there was no stopping my incessant thoughts. Detective Baez had risen to the top.

Though Leesa and Chris had good intentions last night, the attempt at matchmaking could not have come at a more awkward time. Still, I appreciated Andre putting my mind at ease. I had slept a lot better last night, knowing at least somebody at CPD didn't think I was a prime suspect.

"Something has you smiling. I'm glad to see that after your ordeal Monday evening."

I looked up to see Eleanor with her laptop closed shut.

"Hey, Eleanor. You ready for a refill?"

She pushed her coffee cup toward me and placed her elbows on the table. "Sure, maybe I can get my mojo back."

"Oh no! You can't be having writer's block."

She grimaced. "I'm afraid so."

"I will be right back." I grabbed the carafe and made my way over to Eleanor's table. With me being off yesterday, I hadn't asked her about the night Maggie was killed. Now seemed as good a time as any. Careful not to spill the hot liquid, I approached her table. "What's going on?"

Eleanor looked up, her blue eyes twinkling behind her glasses. She pushed her empty cup toward me. "My muse has abandoned me."

"Can't have that now, can we?" I joked, pouring fresh coffee into her cup. I hesitated for a moment before asking, "Did the detectives talk to you about...you know, what happened next door?"

"Detectives? Oh, no, dear. I wasn't near any of the events on Monday night," she replied, shaking her head. "I was at home, working on my latest novel."

I nodded, trying to hide my disappointment. If anyone could have provided some insight on a murder mystery, it would have been our resident author.

"Thanks for the refill, Joss," Eleanor said. "That smile you had on your face a few minutes ago has disappeared. I hope I didn't upset you."

"Of course not," I replied, forcing a smile. "I guess I've been trying to put the other night out of my mind. The detectives talked to me yesterday and let's just say the visit to the police station wasn't pleasant."

"Oh no. That woman is still messing with you even as a corpse."

I cringed. "I guess you can say that."

"Joss," Eleanor began as I was about to walk away.

I turned back to face her. Her tight smile and sharp eyes startled me for a minute. My heart started beating fast. Realizing my hands were shaking, I put the carafe on the table.

"What is it?" I barely recognized my voice, which sounded more high pitched.

Eleanor removed her glasses and rubbed her face. "I know you are on the clock, but it's not that busy right now and there is something I should tell you. I went to school with Maggie."

"Really?" I asked, my curiosity piqued. "I didn't know that."

Eleanor nodded solemnly. "Yes, we were in the same grade. She and her siblings were... Well, let's just say they weren't very pleasant to be around."

"Sounds like they learned a few things from their dad." My voice had an edge to it.

Eleanor looked at me, her eyes sympathetic. "It seemed like the apple didn't fall far from the tree. Maggie, along with her brother, used to torment me mercilessly at school. It was a difficult time for me," Eleanor explained, a bitter edge creeping into her voice.

As she spoke, I couldn't help but imagine young Maggie prowling the school hallways with her gang of siblings, terrorizing anyone who crossed their path. I felt more disgust for the woman who'd been killed next door. No one deserved murder, but she'd not been a pleasant person.

Eleanor seemed lost in thought, her eyes full of an intensity I hadn't seen before. As I watched her, I couldn't help but think back to a few days ago when she'd intervened between Maggie and me.

Maggie, leave Joss alone. You are going to get what's coming to you.

It had seemed like a simple act of defense, but now, with the knowledge of their shared history, it was clear there was more to it than that.

"Hey, Eleanor. You don't have a secret skill, do you? Were you serious when you told Maggie she was going to get what was coming to her?"

Eleanor looked at me, her eyes narrowing slightly. "It wasn't a threat if that's what you're asking. Just... a bit of wishful thinking on my part."

"Uh-huh," I replied. "Well, let's just hope your latest mystery novel doesn't involve a character suspiciously similar to Maggie. People might get ideas."

Eleanor chuckled as she flipped her laptop open. "You never know, Joss. Inspiration can come from the strangest places." Then her tone turned serious. "You know I try not to base my characters on real people." She winked at me and took another sip of her coffee.

"If you say so." I laughed. "Did you ever confront Maggie and her siblings? I mean, you don't strike me as the type to back down from a fight."

"Maybe not now," Eleanor conceded. "But back then, I was younger, smaller, and far less self-assured. Anyway, Maggie may have been a terror when I was younger, but as we got older, things changed. One, I'm a successful author now and I know how to use my words."

I laughed. "I'm glad you eventually found your voice. The world could use more people like you, standing up against bullies."

"Thank you, Joss," Eleanor said softly, her eyes shining. "That means a lot coming from someone as brave as you."

"Brave? Me?" I scoffed, feeling the heat rise in my cheeks. "Hardly."

"Taking on producing a true crime podcast, especially with the topic hitting so close to home," Eleanor replied, a knowing smile on her lips. "You are probably making more of a difference than you realize."

I couldn't help but smile back at her. "Thank you. I appreciate it." I grabbed the carafe and headed back to the counter. Fay eyed me as I moved behind the counter.

With a raised eyebrow, she asked, "Everything okay?"

I sat the carafe on the burner and removed the old filter, so I could start a fresh brew. "I'm not sure."

Fay crossed her arms. "You were talking so long with Eleanor I was wondering if you were helping her plot her next book."

I sighed and looked back over my shoulder.

Either the refill or our conversation must have sparked something because Eleanor was furiously typing on her laptop. Sure, she claimed she never based her characters on real life, but I couldn't imagine a local author with history to the deceased that would ignore the mystery behind Maggie Nelson's murder.

Unless Eleanor was hiding something.

Wednesday, September 14, 2:02 p.m.

Usually Eleanor occupied the corner booth by the window all day. But after the lunch crowd left, I noticed she'd wasn't in her usual spot.

The chimes on the café door rattled, and I turned from where I was stocking cups. Eleanor walked in with her laptop bag swinging over her shoulder. Instead of heading to the booth, she walked up to the counter.

"You're back. I thought you might have packed up for the day."

Eleanor attempted to smile, but she appeared exhausted. "I had a nice spurt of inspiration after we talked, but it left me.

I went for a walk. Do you know what they did with Maggie's cats?"

It looked like I wasn't the only frazzled one. "Um, I don't know. The only reason I went over there the other night was because I saw Trixy standing near the open front door."

Eleanor held her hands over her chest. "Oh, my goodness. I didn't know. I'm sure they didn't leave the cats inside the shop. I have a friend who works at the animal shelter. I can call her."

I realized that even though Eleanor was at the café every day, I knew little about her. In fact, I didn't know if Eleanor was married or had kids. "Do you like cats? Sorry, I didn't know if you had any pets."

Eleanor's face brightened. "I do. I have two cats at home. In fact, my cats came from the same litter with Trixy."

"I didn't know that." I was finding out all kinds of things about Eleanor today. "How did that happen?"

"Maggie fostered kittens. She'd bring them to the shop with her. Trixy and Midnight stayed. She might not have been the best around people, but she loved her cats."

"My grandmother has three cats now." Louise had more cats before a brief stay at a nursing home. One of her cats, a ten-year-old orange tabby, didn't like me, but thankfully I bonded with the two younger tuxedo cats, Mickey and Minnie.

Usually one or the other, mainly Minnie, stayed in the room with me at night.

"That would be wonderful if you, or someone, could give those cats a home."

"I will try to find them," Eleanor bobbed her head.

Something felt off with Eleanor. "Is everything okay?"

She looked at me, her eyes wide. "Have you seen Claude? He usually comes in at this time of day."

I tilted my head, concerned with Eleanor's sudden change in topics. "No. I haven't seen him since Monday afternoon. Why?"

"Because he's been acting strange lately," Eleanor replied. "And truthfully, I'm worried. I know he had his issues with Maggie. I just hope he doesn't get dragged into this mess somehow."

I moved closer to the counter. "Issues? Claude gets along with everyone. He's the nicest guy."

Eleanor sighed. "Yes, he is. He's like his father, who was my dearest childhood friend. I never married nor do I have any children, so I consider Claude like a son. He usually helps me with handiwork around the house when he's not busy painting. But he hasn't returned my calls. Maybe he's caught up with a new masterpiece."

"Well, he's painting a portrait of my grandfather. In fact, I'm supposed to stop by this week to see how it's coming along." Wondering where this conversation was headed, I asked. "Why are you concerned about Claude? I know Maggie sold painting supplies in her shop, but I can't see another reason why they would have any run-ins."

"Oh," she continued, "the last time he came over to help me with something, he told me he'd gotten into an argument with Maggie. Maggie was his landlord. The Nelsons owned, and still own, a lot of property in Sugar Creek. Maggie was planning on kicking him out of his studio apartment because he'd been late paying rent. It wasn't his first time."

I blinked in surprise. "Landlord. I didn't know she owned Sugar Creek Lofts. There are a lot of artists and musicians that use that place."

Claude and my friend Blaze had studios at Sugar Creek Lofts, otherwise known as the Lofts. Built in 1908, the building used to be a textile mill. When I went to visit a few weeks ago, I remember Claude telling me the building had sat vacant long after the textile industry shut down in Charleston.

Eleanor nodded. "Yes, Sugar Creek Lofts used to be Nelson Mills. Maggie's grandfather started the textile mill. I believe it's where the bulk of the Nelson money was earned. When he died, Maggie's father inherited it. But he never knew what to do with it. Because of Maggie's mother's interest in the arts, the building was eventually converted into a place that artists could use and even live."

"I never knew that."

Eleanor replied. "Maggie was the oldest of her three siblings and the one more influenced by the hippie days. I will admit, despite her unlikable nature, Maggie was quite the artist when she was younger. She won a lot of awards for her paintings. But after she married and settled down, all of that stopped. I remembered when their mother died and Maggie had inherited the Lofts. About a year later, she opened Crafty Corner. I also heard that was the year her last child left home too."

"How many children did she have?"

Eleanor furrowed her brow. "Only two were born. I heard she'd miscarried two children. Her oldest boy was killed in a car accident. No one's really heard from the youngest child, her daughter."

"That's awful. Maybe the loss of her son and her daughter not being around had to do with her mood."

Eleanor's eyes flashed with anger, something that still surprised me since I rarely saw her share intense emotions. "I can guarantee Maggie was probably born mean. When you told me about the police bothering you, which is absurd, it made me think about what Claude told me."

"But it was just an argument." People argued all the time—it didn't mean they were capable of murder. Although, Claude did see Maggie come into the café on Monday night and berate me. And, while Claude was the nicest guy I knew, I could see how that might have triggered him.

I knew enough from the true crime shows I watched to know that we were all capable of crossing lines into the unimaginable. What would push Claude over the edge?

"Look," Eleanor said softly. "I don't want to cause trouble for Claude. I'm just concerned because I haven't seen him in a few days."

"He's probably super focused on finishing my grandfather's portrait. We're going to unveil it and hang it up here at the café."

Eleanor smiled. "It's good to know he's working on something special. I feel better not hearing from him. I bet you will be thrilled with how the portrait turns out."

I waved my hand around. "I trust Claude. A ton of his work is already on display in the café."

The door chimes rang and two women walked into the café, giggling together.

Eleanor waved at me. "I should let you get back to work."

Instead of going to her booth, Eleanor left the café. I watched as she passed the front window outside, her head down.

That was kind of weird.

With as cheery a disposition as I could muster, I turned my attention to the two new customers. While working on the two vanilla lattes for the customers, my mind gravitated back to the conversation with Eleanor. I wished she hadn't shared her concerns about Claude. Earlier, I had suspicions about her, which she didn't make any better. Despite the years that had gone by, I could tell there was no love between Eleanor and Maggie.

I knew there had to be people who had beef with Maggie. But I didn't like that it was two people I really liked and admired.

Chapter 9
Something In the Air

Thursday, September 15, 1:05 p.m.

After the strange conversation with Eleanor about Claude, I worried throughout the night. Thursday morning became even stranger. For the first time in a long time, Eleanor wasn't at her usual booth. Sometimes, if it was raining, she wouldn't make it to the café. But it was bright and sunny today.

With her being off her writing game yesterday, I figured maybe she'd gotten sick. I knew this time of year hay fever became a problem for folks with allergies. My grandmother was having a time. She'd sneezed so hard a few times last night that she scared me. We laughed about it, but she had me concerned. These older folks around me had me really pondering getting older.

I guessed Eleanor to be in her late fifties or early sixties. I could never really tell a person's age. I knew people thought I was like nineteen or at most, twenty-one. Definitely not twenty-seven. It's been hard for me to believe too. I spent most of my twenties trying to figure out what I wanted to be when I grew up.

I was still struggling with the adulting part of my life.

After the lunch crowd diminished, I asked Fay about heading over to Claude's to check on the painting. Really, I wanted to see how he was doing. He was another regular who'd been missing in action since Monday night.

"I won't be long," I said to Fay. "I'm wondering if he and Eleanor ever connected." I had been concerned about my conversation with Eleanor and shared my thoughts with Fay. "Do you know where she lives? I don't suppose you have her phone number?"

Fay's glasses hung precariously around her nose. "You are really worried about our resident writer."

I frowned. "Aren't you? I mean, I know Eleanor uses that booth every day like a home office, but she seemed a bit off yesterday. She was so worried about Maggie's cats. I'm also wondering if she was coming down with something and that's the reason she's not here."

Fay nodded. "There's definitely something in the air. Could be sickness. But everyone is also probably freaked out about

Maggie getting killed." She looked around the café, her brows furrowed. "It's been slower the past few days than it has been in a long time."

I'd noticed that too, but I didn't want to say anything.

Fay sighed. "As long as you can be back in an hour. Hailey has to leave for her class."

"Absolutely!" I began pulling off my apron. "I appreciate it." Fay was the best boss I'd ever had. It didn't hurt that she had her own business, so she could do what she wanted. She was very flexible with her three employees.

Fay added, "Let Claude know I asked about him. I can't wait to see his latest masterpiece. I'm sure it's going to be perfect on that wall."

I smiled and turned to the vacant wall space. I felt grateful for all the support I had helping me honor my grandfather. Being one of Fay's friends, Claude's work hung in various corners of the café, but this one would be special.

Thursday, September 15, 1:55 p.m.

I walked over to the Lofts. The center was only about a block away from the café. That's one of things I liked about Sugar Creek, its mixture of businesses and communities. The historical society protected a lot of the buildings.

The reddish brick building loomed ahead of me as I approached. The building's security was pretty high tech despite the historic architecture. There were cameras above the entry door, and a resident's key card was required for entry or a resident had to buzz guests inside.

I went up to the door and pressed the number labeled Claude McKnight. A few minutes later, Claude barked, "Hello."

He sounded salty, and I was a little taken aback. I knew it had to be almost two o'clock.

Oops, I forgot he keeps weird hours.

"Claude, it's Joss. Is this a good time?"

With a bit more softness to his voice, he replied, "Joss, hey girl. Come on up."

There was a loud buzz, and then the entry door opened for me with a click. Once inside, I passed the music studio. It was the first door on the right after entering the building. The window next to the door was dark, so I knew Blaze wasn't around today. I'd spent most of the summer in there while Blaze helped me mix the podcast audio.

I headed toward a dark wooden staircase that creaked with age. I enjoyed running my hands along the shiny banister as I climbed the stairs to Claude's studio apartment.

Most of the studios were outfitted with kitchen and bathroom facilities, but Claude was the only one I knew who seemed to stay in the building twenty-four seven. Probably because inspiration came to him mainly at night. He often slept until early afternoon.

He must have seen me coming on the camera inside his studio. I could hear him disengaging the locks, which still took a bit of effort. I thought this was so strange the first time I came to his studio, but I guess his paintings were valuable.

He poked out his head. "Joss, good to see you. I'm glad you could come by."

Claude appeared like he'd just rolled out of bed, but his eyes were bright as if he at least had been up for a while.

"Are you sure? Fay gave me a break, so I hope it's okay to drop in. If not, I can come back later." Claude rarely looked at his phone, texting him would have been a wasted effort. I grinned. "I was curious about how the portrait was coming along."

He laughed and waved me inside. "Sure thing, come on in."

As soon as I stepped inside, the scent of oil paints and turpentine filled my nose. I'd been here before, so I was used to the smells. I turned to access Claude's tall frame, keeping in the back of my mind some worries Eleanor had expressed.

Other than his scruffy attire, which was not unusual, he looked fine and healthy to me. Claude was at least ten years older than me, but he resembled a surfer boy clothed in a large gray t-shirt and sweatpants. I could tell he'd been caught up in his work because his long brown hair was pulled back into a ponytail. He sported a goatee that could use some grooming, but his blue eyes sparkled. Really, when Claude cleaned up, he was a stunningly handsome dude. With his slim build, he could have been a model.

He clasped his hands together like an excited child. "I'm glad you stopped by." Then his smile slid from his face as suddenly as it appeared. "I wanted to talk to you on Monday about my progress, but then everything happened..."

My shoulders slumped. "Yeah, I know. Maggie happened."

Claude touched my shoulder. "Maggie wasn't a very pleasant woman. Not that I would wish murder on my worst enemy. Come on, let's look at the portrait. I guarantee it will lift your spirits."

I followed Claude over to the corner of the room. We passed by various paintings on the wall which I'd seen before. Claude's work was always a breathtaking experience. His specialty was painting portraits from photos. I loved the warm, but vibrant colors he used to bring the people he painted to life.

He had a few pieces recently sent to a gallery in downtown Charleston and another painting to a gallery in Savannah. I loved how much attention he was getting for his artwork and couldn't wait to share more of his talents with the world.

"Are you ready?" Claude ran his hand over his hair as if he'd just realized he wasn't looking his best.

I nodded, unable to speak, which wasn't normal for me. Usually, when I was nervous, I babbled.

I approached the easel where he'd been working. Almost in slow motion, I turned to face the canvas. My breath caught in my throat when I saw the portrait. It was a beautiful rendition of the picture that showed my grandfather in his baseball uniform at bat. The gleam in his eye and the strength in his stance were so lifelike, I felt like he could leap off the canvas and embrace me.

"Wow, Claude... It's incredible." My voice hitched as tears welled. The flood of emotions surprised me. I guess after everything that happened this week with Maggie, the interrogation and my mother, I felt raw and vulnerable.

"Are you okay, Joss?" Claude asked, concern etched on his handsome features. He strode over to his desk and grabbed a box of tissues. "I hope those are happy tears."

I laughed as I grabbed a few tissues from the box. The joy that bubbled up inside me felt so good. I wiped at my eyes. "I...I just didn't expect to be so moved by this. You've really captured him, you know? He seems so real and lifelike. Thank you, Claude. This means more to me than I can express."

Claude glanced away with a small smile on his face. "I'm just glad I could do him justice. I know how much all of this means to you."

I finally tore my gaze away from the portrait. Though I was grateful to lay my eyes on my grandfather's portrait, I had another reason for stopping by.

"Hey, on another note. I believe Eleanor was looking for you yesterday. Did you all ever get together?"

Claude sighed, his shoulders drooping. "Yes, I saw her on the camera. I really needed to keep working and wasn't expecting a visitor. She's usually at the café so I wasn't sure why she was stopping by."

I frowned. "She seemed really concerned about you. Today, she didn't show up. I didn't realize you two were close. Maybe you can check on her."

Claude's eyes grew wide. "Close? I wouldn't say that. I mean, she and my dad were friends. Really, best friends. They grew up together. I think she feels some obligation to look after me since he passed, but I've told her she doesn't need to do that."

"You must look after her, too. Eleanor said you help her out." I teased. "Sounds like you are quite the handyperson. So many talents."

He chuckled. "It took a long time for this art thing to pay off, you know. So, I took up some skills, learned some basic carpentry from my dad. He was a contractor and I didn't want to hear him talking about me being broke."

"That's good to know." I looked at Claude's desk on the other side of the room. I knew he kept a photo of him and his dad on a side table. That's what drew me and Claude together. We'd both lost our dads. Unlike me though, Claude had lost his mother to a car accident when he was twelve. He was an orphan, and I could see how Eleanor, not having kids, gravitated toward looking out for him.

"So, your dad and Eleanor were in school together. Eleanor was telling me earlier that she went to school with Maggie and that she was a bit of a bully."

Claude's eyes clouded. "My dad talked about that often. Except it wasn't Maggie doing the bullying, it was her brother Rick Nelson."

"Wow, that whole family is something else. You know, the cops questioned me because I found Maggie. It didn't help that she'd been in the café a few hours before and we argued." I admitted.

Claude's eyes widened. "Oh no, Joss. That wasn't an argument. Maggie was just being her usual obnoxious self. They're not trying to pin Maggie's death on you, are they?"

"It certainly felt like it. At least Detective Wilkes was making me sound like the prime suspect."

I'd been joking with Andre last night, but I really hoped the detective would look in other directions for the investigation.

Claude sighed heavily, rubbing his neck as if trying to relieve some tension. "You know, Maggie was just like that. She always had to make her opinions known. I had an argument with her a couple of weeks ago," he confessed.

"An argument?"

Claude avoided my eyes. "The Nelson family owns this building even though the mill closed years ago. You probably know they own tons of real estate. Anyhow, things were tough this past winter. I got behind on the rent, but it was my plan to catch up once I sold a few paintings. The crazy thing was, even after I paid her, she still was determined to boot me out of this place."

I frowned, "But why? You said you caught up on your payments."

"Yeah. She tried to say something about how I attracted too many suspicious people around the place, which made no sense. I'm making a living doing my artwork just like she had customers coming in and out of her craft shop. I don't know, that day she just seemed uptight about something and I was her scapegoat."

"I'm so sorry." I tilted my head as a thought came to me. "What happens to this building now with Maggie...? Well, you know."

His eyes were distant as he considered my question. "I imagine her brother will inherit it," he finally said. "You know he's the car dealership guy with his face plastered on television."

I frowned. Maybe I read and watched too many mysteries, but the person who gained a big inheritance also had a motive. I wondered how well Maggie had gotten along with her siblings. But then I remembered something else.

"But Maggie had a daughter too. I guess they were estranged."

Claude tilted his head to the side. "You know what? That's right. I remember her being a few years ahead of me in school. Maggie's son died. That whole family was meaner than a sack full of rattlesnakes. They never cared about anybody but themselves."

The vehemence in his tone caught me off guard, and I studied him more closely. Maybe Claude was more affected by the Nelsons than I thought.

"What do you think the new ownership will mean for you and all the other artists that use the Lofts?"

Claude sighed, running a hand across his unruly hair. "Honestly, I don't know. I'm not sure I want to find out, either. But I guess we will have to wait and see."

"You know how you said Maggie's brother is probably going to inherit this building? That got me thinking... Do you reckon someone in her family might've, you know, had a reason to want her gone?"

Claude looked at me, his eyes wide. "It's certainly possible. From rumors I've heard, Maggie didn't really talk to her brother. And you know her younger sister went to prison for that fraud scheme. That's why the other day seemed weird with her coming into the café to blast you. I heard she wouldn't even visit her old man when he was in the nursing home."

"Well, he had Alzheimer's. I imagine it would be hard to be around someone who doesn't know you anymore."

"True." Claude looked at me for a few seconds. "I know talking to the police probably scared you, but I want you to promise me something, Joss."

I frowned. "What's that?"

"Promise me you'll be careful," he insisted. "It sounds like you are really curious about Maggie and her family. I don't want anything to happen to you."

I nodded, swallowing the lump in my throat. Claude's warning jolted me and trepidation climbed up my spine. Still, despite my growing fear, my desire to catch the real killer continued to increase. I had no intentions of being anyone's scapegoat.

I just hoped the killer wasn't someone I knew and admired.

Chapter 10

Unwanted Feedback

COLD JUSTICE PODCAST
Episode 3: The Best Friend

Joss: Welcome back to the *Cold Justice Podcast*. Today, I have as my special guest, Sammie Morrison, who was my grandfather's best friend. Sammie, thank you for joining me today.

Sammie: Thank you for having me, Joss. It's an honor to be here and share my memories of August.

Joss: Sammie, my aunts told me that you and August were inseparable. Can you tell me about some of your most cherished memories together?

Sammie: Your aunts are precious to me. And they're right, August and I became friends because of our love of baseball. We not only played the game, but collected and traded baseball cards too. As far as memories, oh, there are so many, Joss.

Joss: August was known for his resilience and determination in the face of adversity. How did his experiences shape his outlook on life and his pursuit of justice?

Sammie: August faced his fair share of challenges, Joss. The discrimination he encountered, especially on the field, fueled his desire for change and justice. He believed in standing up for what was right, even when it seemed impossible. August was relentless in his pursuit of justice, not only for himself but for others who faced similar struggles. He was a fighter. Even in the end, that man never backed down.

Joss: As August's best friend, you must have shared many conversations about his dreams and aspirations. Can you tell us about the impact he wanted to make in the world?

Sammie: August had big dreams, Joss. He envisioned a world where everyone was treated with equality and respect, regardless of their race. He believed in the power of education and music to break down barriers and bring people together. August wanted to inspire others, especially young Black men, to reach for their dreams and know that they could achieve greatness. I was honored to be his friend.

Joss: Sammie, we're here today to uncover the truth behind August's murder. Can you share any information or insights that you may have about that fateful night?

Sammie: Joss, that night... It's etched in my memory. I was with August just hours before his tragic death. We were playing a gig at a local club, and everything seemed fine. But as I left, I couldn't shake this feeling of unease. Something didn't feel right. The people who'd cornered him in the alley had been on him for weeks. But their bullying didn't stop him from going on with his life. I've been haunted by that night and the questions that remain unanswered.

Joss: Thank you for sharing, Sammie. I've appreciated getting to know you. Your stories have brought me closer to my grandfather, even if only through memories.

Thursday, September 15, 6:07 p.m.

Because of the events that happened next door, Fay postponed Friday Night Jam until next week. I guess I should be grateful she didn't cancel it and make us wait until next month. We'd already advertised it and people were used to attending.

I spent the rest of the afternoon in Fay's office contacting singers and musicians. I'd posted new graphics on the café's social media pages with the updated event date information. I never thought I was good at much, but I enjoyed experimenting with templates and customizing graphics for the café. It was fun and relaxing.

While on her computer responding to people on Instagram and Facebook, I took a peek at the Instagram page I'd set up for the podcast. Thank goodness I'd only set up one social media network. It was hard enough to keep up with the comments on one. Plus, the more I scrolled through the comments, the more my mood grew sullen. Social media could be hit or miss with me. I wasn't happy with about a quarter of the comments. It didn't surprise me that not everyone loved the podcast, but there were way too many comments that reflected Maggie's opinion.

Why is this podcast stirring things up in the community?

It's past history. Who cares?

He probably deserved it.

Do you think this has anything to do with Maggie Nelson's death?

Suppose it was a revenge killing.

My mouth grew dry and my body felt flush with anger. People were really speculating about Maggie's death on my podcast's IG page. That was not good!

Did the cops look at this kind of stuff? No wonder Detective Baez decided to listen to the podcast.

Fay entered the small office, startling me out of my thoughts.

She eyed me for a few seconds before asking, "Are you okay, Joss? You look like you are going to be sick."

I gulped and closed the browser window. "I'm fine." I didn't want to share what I'd just read. The café had already suffered enough this week with the lack of business. I forced a smile like I always did. "People are disappointed, but happy that we postponed the jam until next week. A few people thought we should do a tribute to Maggie."

Fay scoffed. "The way she treated you, I don't think so."

"I figure it would take some of the attention off me. Surely the cops can't think I killed a woman and then turned around and celebrated her life." Apparently, some people thought the podcast and Maggie's death were related.

Fay peeked over her glasses at me. "You don't need that kind of attention. I'm sure people are talking enough without us adding to the mix."

I sighed. I knew I couldn't keep anything from Fay. She probably saw the page before I closed the browser. "People are definitely talking on social media."

Fay's eyes were sympathetic. "I figured. You can't let the comments from the Maggies of the world get you down. We'll pray that all of this blows over soon. I'm pretty sure with Maggie being from the infamous Nelson family, there has been some pressure on the police to arrest someone."

I frowned. "I hope it's not me."

Fay shook her head. "They have no evidence."

I pulled off my apron. "Yeah, I guess you're right. I hope none of this, the podcast or Maggie's death, is affecting the café."

Fay crossed her arms. "Yes, I've noticed it's been slow most of the week. Don't think I don't hear you, Briana, and Hailey whispering. Despite everything going on, you girls don't have to worry. The café is in good shape. Actually, Friday Night Jam brings in a good cash flow each month. And you've seen me increasing the baked offerings, even offering breakfast and lunch items."

I smiled. "You are a boss lady. I know things will pick up next week. Good news is the performers I contacted are ready to go next week." I snapped my finger. "I need to check in with Blaze to make sure he can DJ for us since this is off schedule now. You know, he and Sammie have been missing-in-action this week. I wonder what that's all about?"

Fay shrugged. "Well, the gossip train ebbs and flows. There will be something new next week and I expect everyone will want coffee for their soul." Fay waved her hand. "You can head home. Joe is going to come by so we can hit the town tonight for dinner and a movie. He has to go out of town this weekend for a relative's funeral."

I grabbed my bag from my locker and shut it closed. "You're not going with him?"

Fay shook her head. "Um, no. Besides, Joe and I spend every day together. Not to be funny, but a solo Netflix and chill night is on the menu for me."

While I wished I had someone, my relationship goals were batting zero. It always seemed like I was on the opposite end, and here Fay was looking for a chance to spend time away from her man.

I pulled my keys from my bag and called over my shoulder. "I'm heading out."

Fay rose for her desk and followed me up to the front of the café.

I grinned back at her. "Enjoy your night out and your weekend of solitude."

Fay snapped her fingers. "Girl, I plan on it. You have a good night, Joss. And no more looking at those comment sections."

After Fay closed and locked the door behind me, I glanced over at the craft shop. There were more flowers piling up outside the door and someone had set up a candle. I was glad Maggie had some people who missed her.

I just wished she'd left me alone.

Thursday, September 15, 6:21 p.m.

Once inside my car, I didn't start the engine right away. With the jam postponed, my mood had become more unsettled. I wondered if normal would ever return.

I texted Blaze before I forgot.

Joss: We postponed Friday Night Jam until next week. I hope you can still DJ.

He responded a few minutes later.

Blaze: Really? What's up?

Joss: Bad timing. You know... The other night.

Blaze: You at home?

Joss: On my way.

Blaze: Can you drop by? Want to hear more!

I looked at the text message. This wasn't the first time Blaze had asked me to drop by. We mainly hung out in the studio when we worked on the podcast. I'd been avoiding his home base.

But I wanted to check on Sammie.

I started up my car and glanced at the dashboard clock. Blaze's house was on my route home, so it wouldn't be out of the way.

I smiled when I saw Sammie on the porch. It was so good to see him. I grew fond of Sammie after my aunts introduced him to me. Being my grandfather's best friend, he had a plethora of stories to share from their childhood.

Sammie had introduced me to his grandson. Blaze and I kicked it off, but soon fizzled. We had this shaky friendship that was at times awkward, but I was grateful Sammie held nothing against me for breaking up with his grandson. He even hinted to me that Blaze could be a little rough around the collar.

I pulled into the driveway behind Blaze's Dodge Charger. The two-family house had two front doors with the right side leading to Blaze's residential area. The other entrance was Sammie's part of the house. I had grown pretty familiar with the residence years ago, but rarely visited now.

Sammie sat on the small porch strumming his guitar. He gave me a big, toothy grin as I walked up the steps.

"Hey, Sammie. I haven't seen you in a few days. Fay baked some fresh pies this morning."

Sammie smiled. "You know, I knew there was something I missed today. Fay's sweet potato pie reminds me of my mama's cooking."

I grinned. "Well, it was a little slow today, so I'm sure she will have plenty for tomorrow. I'm going to head in to see Blaze. Fay moved the jam to next week. You haven't been in a long time."

Sammie nodded, but he didn't respond. He seemed to drift off, while he absently strummed the guitar. I frowned, thinking either he didn't hear me or forgot I was standing there.

Blaze opened his door suddenly, peering out at me. "Hey, Joss." He glanced over at his grandfather, a worried expression on his face. "Pops, you doing good?"

Sammie blinked. He lifted his face and stared blankly at Blaze. Finally, he smiled. "I'm enjoying this evening breeze."

It was a pleasant evening, and I was glad my curls hadn't turned into a frizzy fro. The summer heat and humidity still liked to sneak in, even though it was after Labor Day. But that was the pleasure of being in the South.

"Pops, let's get you inside." Blaze glanced at me. "Can you stay a minute, Joss?"

I knew I should be going now that I saw Sammie, but I smiled. "Yeah, sure."

Blaze walked Sammie inside, who I guess had grown tired. I waited on the porch for what felt like a long few minutes. I almost started walking to the car.

Blaze came out and waved me toward his door. "Sorry about that. Come on in, Joss."

Against my better judgment, I followed Blaze inside his home, which looked like the typical bachelor pad. A large flat screen television was mounted on the wall and next to his black leather couch, game controllers decorated the coffee table. Unlike other bachelor pads, Blaze's DJ equipment sat in the corner along with stacks and stacks of vinyl's.

Barefoot and dressed in his usual attire of a hoodie and jeans, he turned to face me. His smile made me feel things I shouldn't. Blaze was a handsome guy and he could easily pull any woman he wanted. In fact, when we were dating, I soon learned as a DJ, he had his own set of groupies.

I asked, "So I hope you can emcee and DJ next Friday at the jam. I know you are pretty booked up with other gigs."

"Y'all are in luck. I had a gig out of town, but they cancelled." He took a seat on the couch. "The music community really appreciates Fay for providing a venue to introduce local acts. I will do my best to always be available. Take a load off your feet, I know you've been on them all day."

I sighed and then plopped down in a chair across from the couch. A few summers ago, when Blaze and I dated, I was over at his house so much, my mom had accused me of moving in. Since I had clothes, toothbrush, makeup and everything else over here, I did stay for a few months after my lease expired on my apartment. That was also when I discovered how intense Blaze could be.

I often hung out at the clubs or parties while Blaze DJ'd. What I hadn't realized before then, Blaze had a temper which led to multiple run-ins with other individuals. A man started flirting with me, which wasn't an uncommon thing. But that night Blaze took offense and punched the man in the face. His violence landed him in jail, but the other man decided not to press charges. Things were never right after that with us. While he never harmed me, I didn't feel comfortable in an intimate relationship with him after that. His rage scared me.

But that was the past.

And even though he was the first person to come to mind to help with my podcast, I still tried to keep a bit of distance between us so there were no wrong ideas. I'd gotten in that trap before of going back to an ex when I knew I should have kept it moving.

"I've posted on social media and reached out to all the acts that were on the waiting list the last time."

"Sounds good to me," Blaze said and leaned back on the couch with his hands behind his head. "The jam has been picking up lately. I hate we have to slow the momentum. I assume Fay wanted to let the talk about Maggie Nelson die down."

"You got it." An uncomfortable thought crossed my mind, and I knew I had to address it. "Hey, Blaze, I found out something interesting the past couple of days. Did you know Maggie or at least, her family owned the Lofts?"

Blaze raised an eyebrow, clearly surprised by the question. "Yeah, I knew that. I can't say I was happy about it, but I heard Maggie's mom was into the arts and insisted on having a place that supported the arts here in Sugar Creek. Why do you ask?"

"Sorry," I said, feeling a little embarrassed. "It's just that... Well, the police questioned me like I did her in. She went all ballistic on me because of the podcast, but I figured I wasn't the only one she'd blasted."

Blaze sat up. "I knew the detective talked to you that night. He asked you more questions?"

"Yeah, I had to come in the next day and give an official statement. It turned out to be more of an interrogation by Detective Baez and Detective Wilkes. You know I had a run-in with Wilkes a few years back. She's not pleasant at all. Andre seemed to be okay."

"Andre?" Blaze frowned. "You're on a first name basis with the detective."

I gulped. "I meant Detective Baez. Long story, but we have mutual friends. So I've met him outside of his cop persona."

Blaze's eyes flashed. "You should still be careful. It wouldn't be good for you if you said something to him and he used it against you."

I held up my hands. "Don't worry." I wasn't sure if Blaze was concerned about me or jealous. He seemed to get a bit too hot under the collar with my snafu mentioning the detective by his first name. "I'm pretty sure someone else will come out on top, having it in for Maggie. Did you ever notice any conflicts between her and anyone else?"

Blaze's frown increased in intensity as he seemed to ponder my question. "Claude got into it with her a few weeks ago."

"Did he?" I didn't want Blaze to know that I knew this information. I wanted to hear his take on the argument, especially if he'd heard it.

"Sometimes Claude gets so caught up in painting his masterpieces that he forgets to pay rent on time," Blaze confided. "Maggie came by the Lofts more than once. The last time she came by, I heard her screeching as soon as I opened the door to the music studio. It's soundproof in there, you know, so I don't know how long they'd been going at it. I could tell Claude was livid. I would have been too. She threatened to have him and all his stuff tossed out on the street."

"No way." That was more serious than Claude explained. "She could have ruined some of his work if she did something like that."

Blaze nodded. "Exactly." He shifted on the couch so he could lean forward. "Look, I'm sorry to hear about the police breathing down your back. You've been through a lot lately. How are you holding up?"

"Thanks for asking," I offered him a small smile. "I'm managing."

An uncomfortable silence snuck up between us. It wasn't the first time this had happened. And when it did, I took it as my cue to leave.

I pulled out my phone. "Oh goodness, I need to head home. Louise is going to be looking for me. I really appreciate you being so flexible about Fay changing the date for the Friday Night Jam." I popped up from the chair, my legs feeling a bit wobbly from sitting.

Blaze stood from the couch and quickly stepped up beside me. "Are you sure you're okay?"

"Y-yeah," I stuttered, trying to plaster on a convincing smile. I was a little startled at how fast he crossed over to me. We were so close I could feel the warmth radiating off his skin.

His eyes were super-focused on me. "So, how are things with your grandmother? How does it feel living with her?"

A genuine smile tugged at my lips as I thought of Louise. "Honestly? It feels like home. We get along so well."

"I'm glad you found her. Family's important." His eyes were distant.

I knew how much Blaze cared about his grandfather. Sammie had raised Blaze after his dad killed his mom. Blaze's dad was still serving a life sentence in prison.

We were still a bit too close, so I stepped back. "How's Sammie doing? We missed him at the café this week."

Blaze began, his voice tinged with concern. "Pops has been having some memory issues lately. I've been trying to keep him close so I can keep an eye on him."

"Really?" I asked, my eyebrows knitting together in worry. "How bad is it?"

Blaze hesitated, fiddling with the hem of his t-shirt. "He's been forgetting names and details more often than usual. He wandered around the neighborhood once and got lost." He sighed. "He's lived here his whole life. It's just... hard to see him struggle like that, you know?"

"I had no idea." I knew I shouldn't, but I was a touchy feely chick, even when I shouldn't be. So, without thinking, I placed my hand on his arm to offer comfort. My mind raced with thoughts of Sammie — such a kind, gentle soul — facing the challenges of losing his memories. "Have you considered getting him checked out for Alzheimer's or dementia?"

"Talking to Pops about getting a diagnosis isn't easy," Blaze admitted, rubbing the back of his neck. "He's always been stubborn, but lately... It's like he's scared, you know? Like he doesn't want to face it."

"I'm so sorry. I really appreciate Sammie being okay with me interviewing him for the podcast. I could tell he and my grandfather were quite the pair back in the day."

Blaze grinned. "Yeah, Pop's memories about those days are really good. What happened to August still gets to him after all these years. Pops has never cared much for the police because they didn't convict anyone in your grandfather's death."

"Speaking of the police, did they talk to you or Sammie after what happened to Maggie?"

He sighed, running a hand over his fade. "No, and I hope they don't. It's never a good idea for the cops to come around." The tension in his voice was palpable, and I could see that he was genuinely worried for both himself and his grandfather. "I worry about Pops, you know."

I knew Blaze had his own run-ins with the law too. Another reason why I knew he wasn't the one for me.

"I get it," I said softly, meeting his eyes. "Hey, change of topic," I suggested, trying to lift the mood. "I wanted to say thank you again for helping me with the audio mixing on the podcast. You've been amazing."

Blaze's face brightened, and he visibly relaxed. "Not a problem, Joss. By the way," Blaze added, reaching out to give my shoulder a reassuring squeeze. "I'm proud of you for telling your grandfather's story. It's important that people know about his life and what he went through."

"Thank you, Blaze. That means a lot coming from you." Though his words touched me, his hand on my shoulder felt a little uncomfortable, so I adjusted my bag, shifting it up further on my shoulder. "I better head home."

He dropped his arm and stepped back. "Let me walk you out." Blaze flashed me a friendly grin.

With the sun down, it was considerably cooler, and I shivered a bit until I reached my car. I looked through the passenger window and saw Blaze watching me. I waved at him and then started the car.

Despite his intensity sometimes, Blaze really was a cool guy. It was too bad things didn't work out between us romance wise.

A few minutes later, I pulled up to the house. Louise had left the porch light on for me. My phone buzzed in my pocket. Fishing it out, I saw a notification from my personal IG page.

I'd turned off the settings on my podcast's IG page. Those comments could wait until I could settle myself to absorb them.

My heart dropped when I read the comment from the alert notification.

I don't blame you for what you did. She deserved it!

What? Who posted this on my personal IG page?

I read the name.

Rae Silva.

I didn't recognize the name, and the person didn't have a picture. Ironically, they had a cat for their avatar.

Normally, a real, full name was required for signing up on social media, but often people still hid their identities. Was this Rae Silva a real person?

If so, he or she had crossed the line.

Posting your opinion about the podcast was one thing, but I couldn't have people on my personal page inferring that I had something to do with Maggie's death. A shudder ran down my spine as I tried to shake off the uneasy feeling that threatened to overtake me.

Chapter 11

Nip this in the Bud

Thursday, September 15

When I entered the house, Louise sat in the living room in her recliner watching *Law & Order SVU*. I felt guilty for being late; we usually watched the show together. Then fear replaced my guilt.

Louise looked up as I entered the living room. One of the tuxedo cats, Minnie, was on her lap. "There you are. I was going to ask Eugeena and Amos to help me look for you."

I sat down on the couch, still gripping my phone in my hand. I wasn't sure why, but I felt violated.

The person who posted the comment probably meant nothing by it. Apparently, they were not a fan of Maggie's, but they were slinging my name around like I was a suspect.

Louise sat up, and Oreo protested that she had the audacity to move. "Joss, what's wrong? You look upset."

Normally, I wouldn't share things like this with my grand-mother, but I was living in her house. I also really needed to know what to do. "Someone posted something on social media that got under my skin."

I relayed what it said.

"What? Who in the world would do that? Who's Rae Silva?" Louise's face had turned red. "Call the police. They need to track this person down."

I frowned. "Grandma, it doesn't work like that."

With surprising speed, Louise pushed the lever on the recliner down and sprung up with her hands on her hips like she was ready to fight. "Why not? They have to be a local person, right? I don't understand why people just post anything they want. That person can't get away with it."

I stuttered, "Yeah, you're right. But what good will the cops do?"

She shuffled over to me. "What about the detective on the case? Surely you should let him know someone is trying to smear your good name."

I didn't know if I could handle Detective Baez right now. Still, what else could I do? I slumped on the couch. "Okay, I'll call him, but I doubt he can do anything."

Louise nodded. "I will be right here. If he tries any funny stuff, I will sic Tiger on him."

The image of the fat orange tabby cat attacking Detective Baez almost tickled my funny bone. Then I sobered because I wasn't trying to have me and Louise locked up tonight. "Maybe you should keep Tiger in your bedroom for a bit."

Detective Baez arrived quicker than I thought. Nosy neighbors would notice his dark sedan, but at least it was more discreet than a patrol car.

My heart did a little flip as I took in his strong jawline and those eyes that seemed to see right through me. I really hadn't expected him to make a personal visit after I'd called and left a message about the Instagram comment. It seemed silly to do after I got off the phone.

"Are you going to introduce us?" Louise prompted.

"Um, yeah. Andre... I mean Detective Baez, this is my grandmother, Louise Hopkins."

Detective Baez smiled at me and then turned to Louise. "Great to meet you in person. I heard your interview with Joss on the podcast."

Louise held her hand to her chest. "You did? Well, that's so nice of you to listen."

"It's a compelling story that needs to be shared," he said.

I suddenly wanted to get this over with. "Look, now that I think about it, maybe I overreacted by reaching out to you."

"Joss, you have the right to be alarmed. I take this seriously. We have released nothing to the public about our investigation."

"I know," I murmured. "I believe the timing of the podcast coming out and Maggie's death is not helping me."

"Please, have a seat," Louise gestured toward the couch. "Would you like anything? Maybe some coffee?"

He sat down and smiled up at Louise. "Coffee would be great. Thank you."

Louise winked at me before she left the living room.

I blushed. Louise missed nothing. I messed up by almost calling Detective Baez by his first name. Then my flustering around him probably made me appear like some teenager with a crush.

"Joss," he began, his expression serious. "I've been thinking about your podcast, and I can't help but wonder if it might have inadvertently instigated aggression from someone. Or perhaps it's being used as a smokescreen for a personal vendetta against Maggie."

"Wait, what?" My heart raced as I processed his words. Was he implying that I'd created these problems with the podcast?

"Look," I stammered, forcing myself to sound calm. "I know people are talking and feel the same way Maggie did. I never expected my podcast wouldn't ruffle any feathers. It's a sensitive topic, even today. But I definitely wasn't looking to cause trouble."

"Joss, I'm not accusing you of anything," Detective Baez reassured. "But sometimes when we stir up the past, we uncover things that others would rather keep hidden. It's possible your podcast has done that."

I rubbed my temples. "But those directly involved in my grandfather's case are long gone. It's not exactly a secret that Maggie's father, Chuck Nelson, was the main instigator in the attack on my grandfather. It's all on public record. As well as the fact that he and his buddies were never convicted."

Detective Baez raised his hands in a placating gesture. "I'm just trying to consider every angle. I haven't listened to all the episodes yet. Did you ever mention Chuck Nelson by name in your podcast?"

I shook my head. "No, I mentioned no names at all. I made a choice to do that so I wouldn't cause any trouble. I realize the Nelsons still carry weight in this town. The most important thing was to share my grandfather's story. I didn't want them suing me."

Detective Baez crossed his arms, looking exhausted. "So, Ms. Nelson was upset even though you didn't directly mention her father's name." He looked off to the side for a few seconds as if deep in thought. He turned his attention back to me. "But she's the one who's dead. And someone thinks you did it. Why do you think someone would try to link Maggie's murder to you?"

"I have no clue. Are you going to look into this Rae Silva?"

"I can look into it, but I have to ask who knows about the argument between you and Maggie."

"It wasn't really an argument. She came into the café fussing." I thought about the people I'd talked to the past few days. Fay. Briana. Ms. Eugeena. Louise. My aunts. Leesa and Chris. Eleanor. Claude. Sammie. Blaze.

I put my head in my hands. "I've been running my mouth. I probably messed myself up."

Detective Baez looked at me wearily. "Maybe you should tell me the people you talked to."

I rattled off the list of people I'd just thought of. "But nobody on that list would mean me any harm. Detective Baez, if you talk to them, isn't that going to make me look more guilty?"

"Don't worry. And, call me Andre," he said, flashing me a warm smile.

I narrowed my eyes. "Aren't you on duty?"

He grinned. "Technically, I've been off duty for two hours."

"Okay... Andre." My cheeks heated at the sound of his name on my lips. "Why did you come? You could have sent Detective Wilkes. Something tells me she never takes off early."

"No, she doesn't. And I told you, I want you to reach out to me for anything. No matter how small."

The smells of freshly brewed coffee and warm pastries wafted through the air as Louise entered the living room. I eyed her, wondering how long she'd been eavesdropping. I was pretty sure the former president of the neighborhood association had not lost her touch with gathering information.

"Here you go, Detective. I hope you can help Joss. She's been through enough this week."

Andre's eyes widened. "Wow, that's quite the spread, Ms. Hopkins."

"Call me Louise. Since it seems we're on a first name basis." My grandmother grinned like she'd struck gold.

I caught Andre's eyes as he took a sip of coffee.

While I would never admit it out loud, I was glad he came.

Friday, September 16, 9:08 a.m.

Louise, in her typical fashion, tried to get information out of Andre, which I had to give my grandmother props.

She did that!

Before he left, we found out Andre was a military brat. His mom had a distinguished military career, while his dad stayed home to provide a consistent parental presence for Andre, who was the oldest, and his three younger siblings. I wondered if his younger brother and two younger sisters were as handsome as he.

Andre told us his family had lived overseas in Japan for two years and he'd lived in quite a few states, including Fayetteville, North Carolina, for two years.

While he did JROTC in high school, he opted not to go into the military, choosing instead to attend the University of North Carolina at Chapel Hill to study Criminal Justice. After graduation, he entered the police academy. Like most cops, he worked patrol for a few years before moving into a detective role in the Cold Case Unit at the Charlotte Mecklenburg Police Department. I would have loved to hear more about some of the cold cases he'd run across and why he jumped into homicide, but it was past Louise's bedtime.

After the detective left and I'd settled in my room for the night, my mind stuck on the fact that Andre had stayed so long at our house. Eventually, I zoned back to the reason for the visit.

I hadn't said anything to Andre or my grandmother. I knew both would frown on the idea, but I wanted to dig up more information about Rae Silva. If I hadn't vented to Louise, resulting in Andre coming over, that's what I would have done.

I clicked on the name, so I could view the profile more closely. That quickly became a dead end since the person's profile wasn't public. I scrolled down their public posts, which were mainly the same cat in the profile picture, likely a white Persian, and some random photos of a beach. I wasn't sure if the person lived near the beach or if they had been vacationing. The profile offered no clues to the identity of the person.

That creeped me out because the person made their comments anonymously. They didn't want people to know who they were. Who was hiding behind the name Rac Silva?

I still wasn't sleepy, so I grabbed my pen with the purple ink. I found blue and black ink boring. Then I reached for a notebook I occasionally used as a journal. My therapist a few years ago started me journaling. It worked wonders in the beginning. I poured all my angst about relationships that had gone bad, my mother's disappointment in me, my older brother disappearing from my life and how much I missed my dad into my journal.

While I was confident Andre didn't think of me as a murderer, he still had to solve this case. And he had a colleague who would not take me off the suspect board so easily.

I wished Maggie had stayed over in her own shop instead of coming over to bother me at the café. What was so crazy was I'd never had issues with her before. I guess she never had a reason to blast me. Maggie had to know the story about August and Louise. I guess over the past year, with me living with Louise, people had to know I was her granddaughter.

The product of a forbidden love affair years ago.

Why did Maggie come into the café to pick a fight with me? I doubt she even listened to the podcast. She probably just heard the mention of my grandfather's name and had been triggered.

Did the Nelsons even talk about what happened all those years ago? I can't imagine it was something they sat around the dinner table and discussed.

Maggie should have been deeply upset, just like any other human being with empathy, that her dad had gotten away with murder. Instead, she'd inherited his ugly traits of bullying and superiority.

I'd given Andre a list of names, but Maggie had been cruel to other people besides me. I wrote two names.

Eleanor.

Claude.

Both Sugar Creek Café regulars admitted Maggie had been a problem for them.

While I liked her, Eleanor's words and her odd behavior the past few days had me wondering about her. I thought about Eleanor's habit of visiting the coffee shop, which was pretty routine except for this week. She usually arrived mid-morning after the breakfast crowd and occupied *her* booth. Sometimes she left, I assumed, to stretch her legs, but she wouldn't be gone long. I had the sense that her home was within walking distance because I never saw her in a car.

I drew a line on the next page of my journal.

I wrote 4:00 p.m.

Usually a little before four o'clock, Eleanor packed up her things to head home. On Monday, I recalled looking at the clock behind the counter and noting it was already after four. Eleanor had stayed a bit later than usual, even accepting a refill.

Maggie closed her shop at five. But she didn't do that this past Monday. Instead, she stomped into the café. Which made me wonder when she first heard about the podcast. She had all day to say something to me.

When she came into the café, she practically shoved her phone in my face. How did she find out about the podcast? Was she on social media?

I shifted on the bed and grabbed my phone. I did a quick search to find the Crafty Corner on both Facebook and Instagram. There were mainly graphics with promo codes for deals. I saw no mention of the podcast posted on either page. That made sense because it was her business page.

I found Maggie's personal profile on Facebook, but not on Instagram. I groaned. She had it shut up tight with the privacy settings. There were no posts, just pictures of Maggie with cats.

Eleanor had mentioned that Maggie fostered cats, and there were plenty of pictures of various litters of kittens. I swiped the app closed. To me, her social media profile didn't match the woman. But most people posted what they wanted the world to see on these networks.

What I knew about Maggie, she had routines. Why on Monday didn't she just call it a day and go home like she usually did?

Was there some reason she stayed later? If so, why would she let someone in the shop when normally it would have been closed?

This is where I grew uncomfortable with the two people I jotted down that had conflicts with Maggie. Would either Eleanor or Claude have gone to see Maggie after they left the café?

Eleanor's statement was the most ominous.

You are going to get what's coming to you.

Then there was Claude. Even after he caught up his rent, Maggie had threatened to throw him and his artwork out. He probably would have to find another place in Charleston to set up shop. This city supported the arts. But I knew Claude grew up here in Sugar Creek. He had fond memories of his father and he really loved the Lofts.

But Claude was steaming mad about the way Maggie treated me, too. Suppose he stopped next door and had words with Maggie?

I slapped the notebook shut and returned it to my nightstand. I didn't want to think about Eleanor or Claude as suspects.

With the lamp off, I laid my head against the softness of my silk pillowcase. My jumbled thoughts warred with exhaustion.

Sleep won the battle.

But my dreams tormented me.

Chapter 12

Weird Vibes

Friday, September 16, 10:08 a.m.

Business picked back up on Friday morning. Unfortunately, it was just me and Fay handling the morning crowd. Hailey had class, and Briana had picked up a singing gig in Savannah. I didn't mind the business, especially after downing a cup of joe myself. Well caffeinated, I fulfilled orders until about ten o'clock.

Even though we'd gotten the word out on our social media pages about the postponement, most of the morning customers asked about Friday Night Jam. At least we knew how much the community enjoyed the monthly event. It was a lot of work to coordinate, but I wished we did it more often. There was always a waiting list of musicians and singers who wanted to showcase their talents.

I wiped tables, noticing once again that Eleanor wasn't in her usual spot. I hadn't seen Claude either.

My face must have appeared troubled when I came back around the counter.

"Joss, are you holding up okay?" Fay asked, concern etched on her face. "You're not still looking at the comment section are you?"

"Nope." I'd told Fay about the strange comment first thing when I arrived this morning. I also shared my thoughts about Eleanor and Claude. She'd known them longer than me, and I felt terrible that I'd even considered them suspects.

She eyed me. "You look deep in thought. You're not planning on engaging with that person?"

"Rae Silva." I shook my head. "What can I do, message them and say I didn't do what you think I did."

"Good. Don't invite trouble. I'm sure Maggie did what she did best. She probably made someone furious at her."

I nodded. "I'm sure whoever killed her didn't plan it. I can't get that look on her face out of my mind. She looked really surprised. I guess that person was so angry they couldn't stop themselves from pushing her down or something. Maybe they didn't mean for her to die."

Fay emptied the filter and inserted a new one. "What do they call that? A crime of passion?"

"Yep." I said. "Hey, has Maggie ever approached you before?"

Fay sighed and pushed the button to start the coffee brewing. She turned around and faced me, her arms crossed. "Am I a suspect now too?"

"Of course not. You have a better alibi than me. Joe has your back."

Fay held her hand to her chest and laughed. "I'm just joking. And unfortunately, yes. She's tried to get the café closed down a few times."

My eyes widened, and my heart skipped a beat. "What? Are you serious? When did this happen?"

Fay waved her hand. "This would've been a few months before you started here."

I sucked in a breath. "How did she try to get you shut down?"

Fay shook her head. "She had an inspector sent over. When they got here, they found nothing. We still got an A rating for our inspection. She did that to other people on this stretch, too. There's not a single shop owner who hasn't heard Maggie's mouth."

There goes the suspect list. It could have been anyone on this block.

"By the way," I said. "How did you end up getting your hands on this café?"

Fay hesitated for a moment. "You know, most of the buildings on this block were owned by the Nelsons."

I tilted my head to the side and stared at Fay. "No wonder they could get away with murder. Did that family own everything in Sugar Creek?"

Her face appeared grim. "It seemed like they did. But years ago, after Charles Nelson, the first Chuck died, the family went through some tough times. This café used to be a restaurant, and they placed it up in an auction. It was the perfect spot for me to start my new business."

"If I hadn't told you before, you've done an amazing job with this place."

"Thanks, Joss." Fay peered around, looking almost teary-eyed. "I hated the arts weren't valued in the schools anymore. I wanted to create a space that supported the arts, even if it was just a small corner of the world."

"This place is an inspiration to everyone who walks through those doors. I wish I had more artistic vibes myself."

"Joss, don't sell yourself short," Fay insisted. "You have your own kind of art—your storytelling, your podcast."

"I've never thought of it that way. This week has put a down-er on everything."

Fay touched my shoulder. "Why don't we put thoughts of Maggie and the Nelsons out of our mind? It's the weekend, girl."

"I know, but it would be better if Andre could make progress in the case."

"Andre?" Fay raised an eyebrow.

I slapped my hand across my forehead. "Detective Baez."

Fay teased. "Mmmm. I noticed those sparks between the two of you the first time he came in here." She grinned at me. "Have you thought about the possibility of... well, you know, you and Detective Baez?"

"Really, Fay?" I groaned. "Not you too. Leesa, Chris and my grandmother were all in matchmaking mode this week."

Fay arched an eyebrow and pointed her finger at me. "You can't deny there's something there. Besides, it's past time for you to have a good man in your life."

It was my turn to eye Fay. "How do you know Detective Baez is a good man? You were warning me to get a lawyer earlier this week."

Fay shrugged. "From what you've told me about him, he sounds like he's trying to do his job. Like really investigating and not railroading you into being a suspect. Besides, if he really thought you were a suspect, he wouldn't have been making a house call last night."

"He talked to my grandmother more than me."

Fay laughed. "I bet Louise had plenty of questions."

"Yeah, she practically squeezed his whole life story out of him. Which was pretty nice to hear."

Fay poked my arm. "See! You are definitely interested in him, so stop denying it."

She headed back to her office. I sighed; I wasn't in denial. No one knew better than me how the handsome detective had me feeling all warm and fuzzy inside.

In some weird way, Maggie Nelson had been the source to bring us together.

The door chimes snapped me out of my thoughts. I glanced at the clock on the wall behind the counter, noting it was almost eleven o'clock. The lunch crowd would trickle in soon.

I looked up and saw a woman approach the counter. I recognized her from earlier this week. This time, she wore a bright yellow top and green pants. On most people, the outfit might not have worked, but she pulled it off with her vivid green eyes.

The first time I saw her, I thought there was something familiar about her.

I turned on my friendly barista smile as she reached the counter. "What can I get for you?"

She returned my smile with one of her own. "I think I will have a vanilla latte and a banana nut muffin."

"Good choice." I rang her up her and then quickly prepared her order. When I returned with it, I couldn't help but ask. "Do I know you? You look so familiar to me."

The woman hesitated for a few seconds, like maybe I shouldn't have recognized her. But she wasn't the kind of woman who blended into the background very well. She grimaced slightly, like I'd caught her or something. "You probably don't know me, but I know you."

What?

I tried to maintain my professionalism and not freak out. I stuttered, "R-Really?"

She set her shoulders back, the smile now gone. "I'm Renee. Renee Nelson."

I wanted to melt into the floor.

The last thing I needed was to deal with yet another member of the Nelson family.

Friday, September 16, 11:58 a.m.

A miracle saved me from my impending meltdown. The lunch crowd stormed the café, so I didn't have time to ask questions. Fay came from the back office, her eyes wide at the long line. With the dismal business we'd had the past few days, I knew she had to be relieved.

As I took orders, I observed Renee sitting in a booth.

Why was she here? Did she intend to confront me like Maggie did earlier this week?

While I had my back turned to customers, I blew out a breath so my anxiety wouldn't have me hyperventilating. I mean, I wasn't even sure the woman was related to *the Nelson family*, but something about her caught my attention.

It took thirty minutes before the wave of taking orders, fulfilling coffee requests and packing up lunch goodies slowed. As I wiped off the counter, I recalled my conversation with Eleanor a few days ago.

Maggie had a daughter. That woman had similar green eyes, so they must be kin.

Then the part about her knowing about me.

What did that even mean?

"Hey, Fay," I asked as she filled the glass display with more banana nut muffins she'd made this morning. "Do you know if that woman over there is Maggie's daughter?"

Fay almost dropped the pan of muffins. She sat it on the counter and whirled around to look at me. Today, she was sporting red cat-framed glasses which sat perched precariously on the edge of her nose. "What? I didn't know Maggie had any kids, or that she was married."

I held up my hand for her to keep her voice down. "She's at the corner booth. Anyway, Eleanor told me earlier this week. But she also said the daughter was estranged."

Fay squinted at the newcomer. "I've never seen her before."

I nodded. "She was here on Wednesday."

Fay huffed. "I don't like it. If she causes any trouble, we're calling the police."

"I don't think it will come to that."

At least I hoped.

But the woman was in here for a reason. Maybe she'd been next door at the craft shop and wanted to stop in and get some coffee. The problem was she'd been in here at least forty-five minutes. I fully expected her to be gone by now, but she had pulled out an e-reader.

Maybe she wanted to talk to me.

I decided there was only one way to find out. Fay gave me some serious side eye when she saw me grab a steaming pot of coffee.

"Joss, what are you doing?" she asked.

I smiled. "It's time for refills."

What did she think I was going to do? Douse the woman with hot coffee. It's why our regulars loved to visit us. Our sign clearly said free refills for dine-in customers only.

I approached the booth. Renee must have inherited her looks from her dad's side of the family. While she had her mother's eyes, she looked so different from Maggie, definitely more so-phisticated. Renee's shiny hair flowed down her back and she'd applied makeup to her face.

Maggie may have been pretty when she was younger. Now that I knew more about her, I wondered if life had just taken a toll on her. Something made her mean. It was hard to feel sorry for someone who seemed so bent out of shape about everything.

"Can I top you off?" I asked, doing my best to sound cheerful and nonchalant.

"Sure, thanks," Renee said. She pushed her cup to the edge of the table. I could feel her stare as I poured. I knew I might regret asking, but I couldn't help myself. "So, are you related to Maggie Nelson?"

Renee's expression shifted slightly, and she hesitated before answering. "Yes," her eyes bore into me. "She was my mother."

I met Renee's eyes and the knots in my stomach pulled tighter. Was that animosity in her eyes? Did she come in here thinking I had something to do with her mother's death? I placed the coffeepot on the table so I wouldn't drop it. "I'm sorry to hear about your loss."

"Thank you," Renee replied, her gaze never wavering. "And, like I said, I know who you are."

I felt a wave of cold air from somewhere rush down my spine. That's when I noticed Renee had laid her tablet down on the table. My heart skipped a beat as I peered down at the screen, recognizing the familiar artwork for the *Cold Justice Podcast*.

"I see you're listening to my podcast." I felt the heat rise in my cheeks. "But you still had to dig a little to find out more about me. Like the fact that I work here at the café."

Renee picked up the cup and took a slow sip of her coffee before responding. "My uncle told me it was all my mother raged about before her death. So anything that upset my mother, besides me, struck my curiosity."

I sucked in a deep breath to control my nervousness. "I don't want any trouble with your family. If you're listening to the episodes, then you know I haven't focused on my grandfather's—"

"Killers." Renee finished. "Why didn't you? Seems like that would have made it juicer for the true crime crowd."

I narrowed my eyes. "Because all of them are dead. Plus, this was about remembering my grandfather and what he meant to his family, friends and the community."

Renee nodded. "I admire you. Takes a lot of courage to pull something like this together."

I wasn't sure where this conversation was going. But if Renee wanted to start something, I had a hot coffee pot at my disposal. I changed the subject to something safer.

"Do you plan on taking over Crafty Corner? Your mother seemed to have loyal customers." That's the only explanation I could come up with in my head for Renee's visit.

Renee shot me a look as if I'd suggested something laughable. Then she cackled. "Who, me? No. I'm not interested in that place at all. I'm just here because my dad said I should come."

"Oh." This woman was a bit on the cold-blooded side. I almost felt sorry for Maggie. "I didn't realize Maggie had family. I've never seen you before."

Renee shrugged. "I don't live in South Carolina anymore. My parents divorced years ago, after my brother died. He was their golden boy, an only child for a long time. I popped out as a surprise ten years after him." She turned to look out the window as if she wanted to hide her pain.

Unfortunately, I could see her reflection in the glass. The nervousness I felt a minute ago faded away. She was the sort to come off with a hard edge, probably to hide what was going on within.

I cleared my throat. "I was a daddy's girl. My dad died a few years ago. It's been harder to get along with my mom. Never can seem to do anything right for her."

Renee turned around and stared at me. Her face softened. "Well, Joss Miller, we definitely have something in common there. I always got along better with my dad, too. But even he changed after my brother died. So as soon as I turned eighteen, I was out of here. Now I'm back because someone finally offed my mother."

"Finally." I raised my eyebrow. "You don't sound surprised."

She didn't really sound like a grieving daughter, either.

Renee furrowed her eyebrows. "It was bound to happen sooner or later. I'm just glad I wasn't around to catch the blame."

Now I had issues with my mother, but it would crush me if something happened to her. Renee's bitterness made me ponder if she'd seen her mother prior to her untimely death.

"So what's going to happen to the shop? Surely you can find a buyer for it."

Renee pushed her coffee cup to the side. "Probably. But that's not my problem. I'm sure Uncle Rick will be more than happy to take on that task."

"Your uncle? Doesn't he have enough going on with his car dealership?"

"Apparently not," she replied with a shrug. Her green eyes darkened with irritation. "He's always looking for new ways to expand his empire. That kind of thing runs in the family. I'm just sticking around to see if Mom left me anything in her will. Then I'm heading back to San Diego."

Once again, I couldn't help but feel a slight twinge of sadness for Maggie at Renee's words. It appeared her own daughter cared little for her, only showing up after her death to claim whatever was left behind. Despite this, I knew it wasn't my place to judge. It sounded like the loss of Renee's older brother had upset the balance of the household.

I understood those dynamics from my family.

I cleared my throat. "That makes sense, leaving everything for your uncle to work out since you have your own life in Cali."

Renee revealed a genuine smile. "I do. I actually own a coffee house except mine includes a bookstore. By the way, this is some fantastic coffee." She looked over at the sign that hung above the counter. "Coffee for the soul. It's been a pleasure sitting in here, very cozy. And I love the artwork."

I nodded. "My boss Fay is an artist herself. She's really big on supporting the arts."

Renee stuffed her tablet in her bag. "Wonderful. I'm glad I came by."

I frowned. Did she come in here to spy on me? If Maggie was complaining about my podcast to her family, did all of them hate me for bringing up the past? It hadn't even occurred to me that I would come under scrutiny from the Nelson family.

"Is there some other reason you came in here?"

Renee's eyes pierced me as if she was looking through to my soul. "There's no need to worry about me. I think you're cool! I have a lot of folks in my family who like to blast hot air. My uncle... Now he's the one you need to watch out for."

And with that statement, Maggie's daughter strolled out of the café. Flabbergasted, I wasn't sure how long I stood there before I returned behind the counter and placed the coffeepot back on the burner.

Fay had finished replenishing the baked goods behind the glass display. She stood up and looked at me.

"Are you okay?" she asked. "I can't believe you went over there to talk to her. What did she say? You look shell-shocked."

I crossed my arms over my chest. "That was a weird conversation. I'm not sure if I should be relieved or scared." I filled her in on my conversation with Maggie's daughter.

Fay shook her head. "Sounds like Maggie was just as awful to her flesh and blood. Think about what you've learned about Chuck Nelson and all his hateful ways. That stuff gets learned and passed down through the generations. Sounds like Renee was one of those kids who railed against all that toxicity and decided she wanted nothing to do with it."

I rubbed my arms as if I'd caught a chill. "Probably good she moved across the country. Renee seemed nice on the surface, but I have a feeling things were probably really nasty between her and her mother." I cocked my head to the side as a thought occurred to me. "I wonder how long she's been in town."

Fay raised an eyebrow. "You're thinking mother and daughter had some kind of confrontation earlier this week?"

"It's possible. She certainly was bitter enough, and the will seems to be her main concern."

Fay shook her head. "Was that her only concern? While I appreciate that she liked the coffee, I doubt she came in here to do a market study of Sugar Creek Café."

"No, probably curious about me. I guess people are talking about me. Do you suppose that's why business slowed down earlier this week?"

Fay held up her hand. "I'm sure the murder next door had people pausing. But people know you. You really took on coordinating Friday Night Jam and you're well known in the music and artist community. The podcast elevated you and people see you doing good things."

I sighed and closed my eyes. "It's messing with my head. I don't want people thinking I'm some vigilante."

Fay stated, "Maybe you should stay off social media for a while."

I threw up my hands. "You're probably right. Hey, what do you think Rick Nelson will do with the shop next door? It's not like he's going to run it."

Sadness crossed Fay's face. For a brief second, she looked ready to cry.

I reached over and touched her arm. "Are you alright?"

"No. I'm not. I hate to say this, but Maggie's death isn't good for this café or any of the businesses on this street. I've heard that Rick Nelson is more than just a shrewd car salesperson."

I nodded. "Her brother strikes me as the consummate businessperson."

"More like ruthless." Fay said as she grabbed her empty pastry pans and headed to the back.

He's the one you need to watch out for.

Renee's ominous warning still rang in my ears. I wondered if the small suspect list I'd started included a family member.

Chapter 13
Tasty Encounters

COLD JUSTICE PODCAST
Episode 4: The Teacher

Joss: Welcome back to the *Cold Justice Podcast*. Thank you for joining us for Episode #4. I have a very special guest with me. Esther Gibson was August Manning's former teacher. Ms. Gibson, thank you for joining me today.

Esther: Thank you for having me, Joss. It's an honor to share my memories of August with you.

Joss: Ms. Gibson, you had the privilege of teaching August Manning. Can you tell us a little bit about him as a student and what he was like in the classroom?

Esther: August was an exceptional student. He possessed a hunger for knowledge and a genuine curiosity about the world around him. He was diligent, respectful, and always eager to learn. To this day, I still remember that little boy who excelled on every test and had a thirst for learning.

Joss: My grandfather's love for baseball was well-known. He was in your fifth grade class, which was also the same year he started playing. How did he balance his schoolwork and playing sports?

Esther: August's passion for baseball was contagious. He would often incorporate the sport into his assignments and projects, finding creative ways to bring his love for the game into the classroom. August's dedication to baseball and his dreams of becoming the next Jackie Robinson fueled not only his ambitions, but inspired his peers too.

Joss: August's murder was a devastating loss for the community. How was the community affected?

Esther: The community had great hopes for August. Everyone recognized his incredible talent and believed he had the potential to make a significant impact, both on and off the baseball field. August represented more than just a talented athlete; he was a symbol of hope and progress.

The community saw in him the possibility of breaking barriers and challenging the racial prejudices that plagued society at the time. I would say his loss broke a lot of people's dreams and hearts, even their spirits. Many people were afraid anyway during those times, and his murder seemed to compound that fear even more.

Joss: Thank you, Ms. Gibson, for sharing your insights and memories of August Manning. Your perspective as his former teacher provides valuable insights into his character and the impact he had on those around him.

Saturday, September 17 at 2:36 p.m.

My grandmother's voice broke through my thoughts. I moved off the bed where I'd been sitting since getting dressed. After the week I had, I needed this. Time to be around people I loved while eating good food.

When I reached the bottom of the stairs, Louise looked up at me. "Are you okay?"

"I'm okay. Let's get next door. I'm starving."

"That's my girl!" Louise beamed.

I didn't want Louise to know all the thoughts running through my head. Meeting Renee Nelson yesterday had made me more anxious. What were her true intentions? And what would happen if Maggie's brother paid me a visit too? Did he feel the same way about the podcast as his sister?

It was like this dark cloud lingered over my head, taking away from all the things that I wanted the podcast to do. It wasn't fair.

As we crossed over to the yard next door, I took a deep breath inhaling the mouthwatering scents of fish frying and food grilling. The atmosphere was buzzing with laughter and conversation as the Patterson and Jones family gathered for Aunt Esther Gibson's birthday celebration.

Eugeena and Amos always had family get-togethers, especially after church on Sunday. They celebrated all the holidays and everyone's birthday. It made living with Louise even more appealing.

The festivities reminded me of how it used to be when my dad was alive. When my mom would laugh and my older brother would cut up and play pranks. But those were all distant, sometimes painful, memories now. Being around my grandmother, Eugeena and her family had filled in some of those empty gaps.

I tried to talk my mother into coming, but she wasn't interested. Aunt Ruth and Aunt Thelma wanted to come, but they had some obligations at church. They'd mailed their former teacher a gift.

"Joss, dear, let's go talk to Esther first." Louise suggested.

"Great idea." We wove through the crowd of family and friends toward the lady of the hour.

Esther sat in a wheelchair, but I could tell she was a tall woman. Even while sitting, she exuded strength and wisdom.

"Happy Birthday, Ms. Esther," I called out as I neared her. She turned toward me, her eyes lighting up. "Joss and Louise. So glad you could make it."

We both bent over to give her a hug.

I stepped back. "I wanted to thank you again for being on my podcast. It really means a lot to me."

"Of course. It was my pleasure." Esther chuckled. "Thank you for explaining to me what it was. I'd never heard the term before, but sister Cora played it for me the other day. I understand you must have thousands of listeners."

I scrunched up my face. "More like hundreds, but at least people are listening." I watched the data almost every day now.

Esther held out her hand and touched my arm. "It's wonderful that you're telling your grandfather's story. He would've been so proud of you. I think she takes after him. What do you think, Louise?"

My grandmother beamed up at me. "Yes, she does. She's got his charisma and gumption."

These two women were about to have me melt into a puddle out here on the grass. "Thank you, Ms. Gibson. And Grandma." Their encouragement meant the world to me, especially after all the drama surrounding Maggie's death.

I leaned toward Louise. "We should probably get some food. Happy Birthday, again."

"Thanks, Joss." Esther grabbed my hand before I could walk off. Her grip was surprisingly strong for an eighty year old. "I heard about Maggie. Sometimes people just can't face the truth, but you do what God placed on your heart to do. We're all praying for you."

"Thank you," I murmured. I needed all the prayers I could get.

I wandered toward the food and grabbed a plate. It was hard to choose, but I settled on piling my plate with fried fish, hush puppies, and a generous helping of coleslaw before making my way to the picnic tables.

"Joss! Over here!" Leesa waved at me from across the yard. Her and Chris were sitting together.

"Hey, y'all." I plopped down next to them, setting my plate on the table. "This spread is lit!"

"Right?" Leesa laughed. "My mama and Amos don't mess around when it comes to food. Wait 'til you see the cake. It's Aunt Esther's favorite."

"Oh my goodness. I hope I can save some room."

Chris laughed. "I'm sure Eugeena and Amos won't mind you grabbing some take home plates."

"True that! Hey, Chris, thanks for hooking me up with Officer Lyons. I was a little worried at first, because he wouldn't hardly answer my questions. But once he warmed up, it was like he'd been waiting to get the story of finding my grandfather off his chest after all these years."

At the time of my grandfather's murder, Officer John Lyons was the only black officer on the force. And he was the first on the scene after someone anonymously reported finding my grandfather's body. His interview had me more choked up than I expected.

Chris nodded. "I'm glad I could help out. I listened to that episode the other night. That had to be the hardest one to record."

I swallowed my food before answering. "Yes, I expected some emotions when I interviewed Louise, my aunts, and even Sammie. But... no offense, but I always think of law enforcement as being cold and hard. Like nothing affects them."

Leesa said, "That's because there are so many bad apples in the media. But my Chris here and Amos are good cops."

Chris added, "Well, we're not the only good cops."

I noticed Chris looking past me.

Puzzled, I turned and saw the familiar figure of Detective Baez shaking hands with Amos.

My heart skipped a beat.

Despite my circumstances, the detective's presence was growing on me.

Saturday, September 17 at 3:01 p.m.

I turned around to find both Leesa and Chris grinning at me. I narrowed my eyes. "It looks a little suspicious to see Andre here."

"Look at her on a first name basis," Leesa teased.

I slapped my forehead. I wished that man never encouraged me to call him by his first name.

Chris shrugged. "The man has gotta make friends somehow, right?"

"Right," I smiled.

Andre strolled up to the table, his dark eyes meeting mine with a hint of a smile on his lips.

I was definitely not mad about seeing him in those jeans. They looked even better on him than the suit.

"Joss," he greeted warmly.

"Andre." I said sweetly, ignoring Leesa and Chris eyeing us in the background.

"Hey, man," Chris stood. "Let's get you a plate so you can join us."

Andre grinned. "Absolutely. Thanks for introducing me to Detective Jones. He encouraged me to try his fish. It sure does smell good."

I watched Chris walk Andre over to the table of food.

"Ooh, someone's got it bad for Detective Baez! Or should I say... Annndre." Leesa poked me in the ribs. "You might have found yourself a keeper."

"Ouch, girl," I laughed rubbing my side. "Okay, I know you are in your romance phase with all this wedding planning, but what makes you say that?"

Leesa raised an eyebrow. "You can't take your eyes off him and he made a beeline straight to you when he got here."

I grimaced. "He's probably just keeping an eye on his number one suspect."

Leesa crossed her arms. "Now you know Andre doesn't believe you did anything to Maggie Nelson. I heard from Chris that Andre made a case in front of Detective Wilkes about making sure they don't zone in on one person."

That's good to know.

"Well, there are other people who had beef with Maggie."

Leesa tilted her head. "Why are you sounding like my mama? You haven't been investigating on the side have you?"

Ms. Eugeena was known for putting her nose into investigations, and I admired her for that.

I shrugged. "I wouldn't call it investigating, but I have picked up a few things here and there."

"A few things like what?" a male voice inquired.

I jolted. Leesa and I had been talking, so I didn't notice Andre and Chris return. I couldn't tell if my stomach started doing somersaults because of his proximity or because he might have overheard us talking.

Leesa didn't give me time to recover. "Joss has been looking into who else might have killed Maggie."

I protested. "I have just been asking questions."

Andre sat down and his brows furrowed together in worry. "That's not a good idea. Have you read any more interesting feedback on Instagram?"

"Girl, you need to stay off IG!"

"What going on?"

Leesa and Chris were talking over each other at the same time.

Instead of answering, I sighed and took out my phone. After opening my Instagram app, I scrolled to the post with the comments and turned my phone so Leesa and Chris could read it. I had been guilty of looking at the post several times.

Chris looked up at Andre. "Why would this person assume Joss did it? That's dangerous to spread a lie like that."

"Yeah, tell me about it," I deadpanned.

Andre nodded. "I agree. Can't you just delete the comment? We have screenshots of the person's profile."

"If I deleted that one, I would have to delete almost a third of the comments. That one was the only one that flat out stated I must have killed Maggie. The other ones... Well, I'm sure those are from people who obviously haven't listened to the podcast."

Leesa touched my arm. "Like Maggie Nelson. She should have just left you alone."

"How I wished. Do you think her killer could be someone I know?"

Andre shook his head. "It may not be someone as close as you think, but you never really know the people around you either. I've been looking at your Instagram page. The folks making those comments are cowards."

"You're right, Andre. But y'all are talking about creepy stuff, and this is supposed to be a birthday celebration." Leesa clasped her hands to her chest. "You don't really think someone is going to bother Joss, do you?"

I looked on as Andre exchanged looks with Chris. They both might have been off duty, but I could tell they hadn't turned off their detective mode.

Finally, Andre looked at me. "You should still be careful. And let me know immediately if you receive any other messages or anything else strange happens."

"What if I told you I ran into someone interesting yesterday?"

Now all of them — Leesa, Chris and Andre were looking at me. "Who?" They asked at the same time.

"Apparently, Maggie's prodigal daughter, Renee Nelson, is back in town. Of course, she would be here for her mother's funeral."

Leesa leaned forward. "Did she say something to you?"

"Not at first, but she showed up at the café on Wednesday. I thought she looked familiar, but didn't think anything of it. Then she came in yesterday, and this time it felt like she wanted to make her presence known. She knew who I was, and she was listening to the podcast."

Andre pushed his plate to the side. "So what did she say to you? Was she confrontational?"

I shook my head. "No. That's what was so weird. She's been estranged from Maggie, I guess since she left Charleston. She told me after her older brother died, everything in the house changed."

Leesa raised an eyebrow. "She told you all of this?"

"Yeah. She was really candid, like TMI. But the creepy part is it was like she expected her mother to lose her life at some point. That really shocked me. She said she came in from California because her dad told her to come and she wanted to hear her mother's will."

"That's cold!" Leesa sat back.

"Wow," Chris shook his head.

Andre stared at me, his eyes definitely intrigued. "So, you're thinking the daughter could have done something to her mom?"

"Or the brother," I leaned in. "Did you know Rick Nelson inherits everything Maggie owned, like the craft shop and even the Lofts?"

Leesa sucked in a breath. "Wait a minute. She owned Sugar Creek Lofts. How did she get her hands on the arts community center?"

I said, "It belonged to her mother. Actually, it used to be Nelson Mills. So it's been in their family a long time. I'm not sure how the siblings split up the family properties."

Chris stated. "If the mother owned the Lofts originally, then maybe she passed it on to Maggie in her will."

I nodded. "That makes sense."

Andre took a sip of his ice tea before commenting. His face looked troubled. "You have been doing your homework. Like I said, you should be careful. You could set off the wrong person."

Chris added. "Yeah, like a powerful person. Rick Nelson is one to watch because he's well connected with folks like the mayor."

Andre added. "And the police chief."

That's when it dawned on me. "So you all have been getting pressure from Rick. I guess he's breathing down the chief's neck about Maggie's death. Funny, because I heard him and Maggie didn't get along either."

Andre nodded. "We've heard the same. But, despite whatever went on between them in the past, he's the overly distraught brother right now.

Great! That's not what I need to hear.

Between Fay's worry and now what Andre confirmed, the last person I wanted to run into was Rick Nelson.

Thankfully, at that moment, Ms. Eugeena rolled out a large sheet cake. I didn't think I would have room to eat any more food, but somehow the calories I'd consumed disintegrated with all this talk of the Nelsons.

I was too tired of dealing with that family.

We all sang "Happy Birthday" to Ms. Esther. Despite being in the wheelchair, she helped cut the cake. As we settled back at the picnic tables with slices of cake, I couldn't help but steal glances at Andre.

He and Chris had moved over to where Amos and other men in the family were discussing the football season. Apparently, there was a game tonight. I enjoyed seeing Andre at ease among the other men, laughing and joking like he'd known them all his life.

Andre must have sensed me staring at him. He caught my eye and winked, causing a shiver of excitement to run down my spine. I grinned like an idiot before turning away. I looked down at my phone finding nothing in particular to look at.

Maybe Fay and Leesa were right—maybe I would find something special with the handsome detective.

Only time would tell.

Chapter 14

Trouble Brewing

Monday, September 19, 9:04 a.m.

It'd been one week since I found Maggie dead. And despite the good time I had this past weekend, a dark cloud still loomed over my head. Until the mystery of Maggie's death was solved, it was going to be a struggle.

Eleanor had returned to her usual spot. I brought her first round of coffee along with a cream cheese pastry. "It's good to see you. Are you doing okay? I was worried about you." I asked as I set the tray down near her laptop.

She beamed at me. "Yes. I'm sorry. I didn't mean to worry you. I got in touch with my friend at the animal shelter. Trixy and Midnight are settled in at my house now. That's why I've been away. There was no point in trying to write the past few days."

"Really? That's some awesome news for this Monday morning. So are all the kitties getting along?"

Eleanor laughed. "I think after a while everyone will be on better terms. You know cats."

I nodded. "They can be pretty territorial. Did you ever talk to Claude?"

She nodded. "Yes, he came by on Saturday and helped me with my cat door. Since I'm out of the house most of the day, I want the kitties to be able to enjoy my back yard. Come and go as they please. Now, dear, I'm doing all the talking. How have you been? I know this past week was awful for you."

"I'm praying for a better week. By the way, I met Maggie's daughter last week."

Eleanor sat back, her eyes wide behind her circular glasses. "I've never met her. I only remember her son because I taught him one year when I was still teaching English at the high school." She raised an eyebrow. "What did she want? Don't tell me she continued what Maggie started."

I shrugged. "She came in the café looking for me. It was a weird conversation. I don't think Renee really liked her mother, or at least that's how she came off to me."

"Mmmm." Eleanor crossed her arms. "I'm not surprised. That whole family seems to have missed the boat on being civilized or even understanding the golden rule of treating your neighbor as you want to be treated."

I looked around to see who else was sitting near Eleanor before stepping closer. "I received several warnings, even from Renee, to watch out for Maggie's brother. You knew him. Would he really make a big fuss about Maggie's death?"

"Oh my!" Eleanor drew up tall in the seat. "Maggie could be very vocal and annoying, but she mostly stayed to herself. Rick, on the other hand, was and still is that classic jock from school who always had to be the center of attention. He sucked people in with his charm, but he was just as much a snake as his dad. Even more sneaky because of the charm thing. Hopefully, he won't bother you. There's no need, anyway. You just happened to find Maggie's body."

"Sometimes I wished I'd found her sooner. Maybe she would have still been alive." I sighed. "Other times I wished I just went on to my car. But then who knows what would have happened to Trixy and Midnight?"

Eleanor gave me a warm smile. "I know. You saved those fur babies. And that was a good thing."

"Thanks, Eleanor." I turned toward the front of the café. "I should get back over there and help out."

Briana was working today, and we both took turns at the register, fixing orders and wiping down tables. I cleaned up the cream and sugar sidebar and was heading into the back when the door chimes signaled another customer's arrival. I quickly put the dish rag in the laundry pile and washed my hands.

When I came around the corner, I almost stopped dead in my tracks. The man who stood on the other side of the counter stared back at me. For a brief second, I thought about turning around.

Was he here to cause trouble?

I certainly hoped not. As a local celebrity, he was recognizable, thanks to his flashy TV commercials and larger-than-life personality for Nelson Car Dealership. Seeing him up close, I was pretty sure his hair wasn't real, especially the blond part above the graying temples.

I took a deep breath and walked up to the counter. In the back of mind, I prayed.

Lord, please help me. Protect me from whatever is about to come my way.

"Good morning. What can I get for you today?" My smile was so forced, I felt the strain on my cheeks.

Rick Nelson was also the spitting image of his dad.

My grandfather's murderer.

Those piercing green eyes ran in the family.

"Morning," he boomed. "What a nice little place."

From the side, I glimpsed Fay coming from the back office.

"Coffee for the soul!" I stated.

If he even had one.

My nerves were on edge from my head down to my toes. Why would Maggie's brother suddenly decide to grace Sugar Creek Café with his presence? I was surprised he didn't show up last week.

Fay had walked up to the other side of the counter, busying herself with arranging the baked goods inside the glass display. To be honest, the fact that my boss came all the way from the back added to my nerves.

That meant Fay was nervous about Rick, too.

"I'd like to try an espresso," he said, flashing me a charming smile that probably sold more than a few cars over the years. He peered over at the glass display, briefly glancing at Fay. "Is that sweet potato pie?"

Fay nodded. "Yes, would you like a slice?"

He grinned. "Absolutely."

"Coming up." I rang up his order, and he swiped his card.

I glanced at Fay.

So far, so good!

But like his niece the other day, I knew Rick wasn't in here just because he wanted to try our coffee. He was taking his sweet time. So something was up.

I quickly prepared his espresso, while Fay sliced the sweet potato pie. My mind raced with questions. Was he here to confront me about Maggie's death? Did he have thoughts about the podcast like his sister?

"Here you go," I said, handing him the steaming cup and container with the pie.

I'd packed it to go because I thought maybe he would leave, but he didn't. He grabbed a table in the middle of the café and sat.

I looked past him and noticed Eleanor's eyes were riveted on Rick. Did seeing him in the flesh bring back old, forgotten memories for her?

As if he'd just recognized her, Rick called out. "Hey, Ellie, long time no see!"

Other patrons turned to look at the man who'd started a conversation from the center of the café.

"How's your latest book coming along?" he asked.

Eleanor shut her laptop, her eyes narrowing slightly. "Hello, Rick. It's going well, thank you. What brings you here?"

I couldn't help but watch their exchange. Knowing the history between them, I felt bad for Eleanor. I looked to my side, and Fay had moved beside me.

She hissed. "This is not good. Why didn't he take his food to go? Better yet, what did he really come in here for?"

I shrugged. I had no idea, but inquiring minds wanted to know.

"It's been a hard week." Rick announced.

Eleanor nodded solemnly. "I'm sure it's been tough for you and your family. I'm sorry for your loss."

"Right." Rick took a sip of his coffee, his expression unreadable. My intuition told me there was more to this interaction than met the eye.

I bit my lip, trying to figure out how I could join the conversation without making my intentions too obvious. Then, I did what I did best.

Be direct and stick my nose in.

The opposite of what Andre told me to do over the weekend. But I'd rather not be sideswiped by Rick like his sister did to me last week.

I grabbed my usual prop, the coffee pot. Time for refills.

"Excuse me," I said softly, approaching between the two tables. "I couldn't help but overhear your conversation, and I just wanted to offer my condolences about Maggie too."

Rick turned his gaze toward me, his eyes appraising me for a moment before he flashed his trademark salesperson smile. "Thanks, I appreciate that." But there was something off about his tone, and his smile didn't quite reach his eyes.

"Will you be keeping the Crafty Corner open?"

Rick shrugged, taking a sip of his coffee. "I haven't decided yet. I have my hands full. Why, are you interested?"

"Oh no. Crafts aren't my thing. But it would be nice to know if we're going to have a new neighbor."

He sat down his coffee cup. "Truthfully, I haven't really thought that far," he admitted.

"Of course," I replied. I had a feeling he had dollar signs in his head all the time. I wasn't buying that he didn't know what he wanted to do with the place, at all.

I smiled. "That makes sense. It just seems like Maggie had so many loyal customers—it would be a shame to see the place closed down."

Rick took another slow sip from his cup, his gaze never leaving mine. "Yeah, well, I guess we'll have to see what happens once they find out who killed my sister. The police are dragging their feet. It's almost like they don't care."

I frowned, trying to decipher the look in Rick's eyes. Was he suspicious of me? I shook my head slightly, hoping I was just imagining things.

"It's Joss Miller, right?" Rick's eyes were still locked on mine.

I could see Eleanor shift in the booth out of the corner of my eye. "I guess you've listened to the podcast too, like your sister."

"It's been very informative." He stood up from the chair and flashed me the same smile I'm sure he used to sell a car.

So what was he trying to sell me?

"Interesting how a young person like you is diving into ancient history. Seems like you would be more into making Tik-Tok or YouTube videos. That's what my grandkids do, at least."

"Well, I never got to know my grandfather. This was the best way to learn more about him."

"Smart girl." He smiled. "Ellie, so good to see you. I will be on the lookout for the next book. Y'all be good now."

I watched as the door closed behind him, my mind racing with questions. Why had he mentioned my podcast? What did he really think about it?

Monday, September 19, 11:02 a.m.

The sudden sound of the coffee grinder startled me out of my thoughts. I glanced over to see Fay's stormy face. She'd also been watching Rick's exit out of the café.

I walked over. "Are you okay?"

"He's up to something," she huffed. "He has some nerve coming in here. I watched him looking around the place."

"Maybe he was admiring what you did in here," I suggested.

"Please," Fay scoffed, rolling her eyes. "He came in here with an ulterior motive. "

"What do you think he's really up to?" I asked.

"Who knows?" Fay replied, her voice laced with bitterness. "But mark my words, Joss, that man is trouble."

As I mulled over her words, I couldn't help but acknowledge the nagging suspicion at the back of my mind. "Could he be involved in his own sister's murder somehow? She had to have had an argument with someone. Someone shoved her down, maybe not even meaning to kill her."

Fay shook her head. "I've never seen Rick in this café for the entire six years we've been open. I didn't tell you this last week, but when this place was auctioned, he was not pleased I'd won the bid."

"Why didn't he bid on it?"

Fay shook her head. "That's a good question. He will probably inherit everything, including Maggie's craft shop. I wouldn't put it past him to try to acquire the whole block if he could." Fay's eyes narrowed as she glanced out the window. "Including this café."

I sucked in a breath. "For what? Another car dealership. Besides, he can't do that to you and the other small business owners around here. He would hear from the community." A community that had remained over the years predominantly people of color.

"I doubt he would care." Fay looked at me intensely. "I saw you talking to him. He pretends to be nice, but he's not."

"Wait a minute," I stammered, the words tumbling out before I could think them through. "But, Fay!" I grabbed her sleeve to get her full attention. "Answer me. Do you think it's possible... that he had something to do with Maggie's death? To get control over her shop?"

Fay's eyes grew wide. "I don't think he would go that far, but then I wouldn't know. But, Joss, your obsession with this is scaring me a little. Promise me you'll be careful, Joss. I've got a bad feeling about this whole situation."

"I promise," I assured her.

"Good," she said. "Now let's get back to making coffee. We have to get ready for the lunch crowd."

I promised Fay I would be careful, but that didn't mean I would not try to figure out what Rick was really up to.

Not only had Rick's niece warned me, but Andre hinted Rick had been causing problems for his boss, which naturally trickled down to him and Wilkes.

Sounded like there could be more disastrous results because of Maggie's death.

There was nothing I could do about past run-ins with the Nelson family, but I intended to stop this Nelson from ruining anyone else's life.

Chapter 15

Double Doubts

Tuesday, September 20, 9:40 a.m.

I looked up to see Detective Andre Baez walking into the café, his eyes meeting mine. A flutter of excitement tickled my stomach as he approached the counter. I smoothed down my apron, trying to suppress the grin that threatened to spread across my face.

Calm down, girl!

"Detective Baez," I greeted him. "What can I get for you today?"

"Hey, Joss," he replied. "I'll take a black coffee, please."

"Coming right up," I said, turning to prepare his drink. As I worked, I couldn't help but steal furtive glances in his direction. There was something about Detective Baez that intrigued me, besides the fact he was tasty to look at.

The warmth of the coffee cup seeped through my fingers as I handed it to Andre. Our fingers touched briefly during the exchange. I put my hands down by my side, feeling a bit electrified from our fingers brushing.

"So, any updates on Maggie's case?" I asked.

Andre's gaze lingered on me for a moment, as if he wanted to tell me something. He sighed and set the cup down on the counter. "Joss, you know I can't discuss ongoing investigations."

"Fine, keep me in the dark then," I said with a playful pout, my eyes narrowing slightly as I feigned frustration.

Andre chuckled. "I really enjoyed seeing you at the birthday celebration this past weekend." He took another sip of his coffee, eyeing me over the rim of his cup.

My cheeks flushed at the compliment, a rush of excitement coursing through me like a jolt of caffeine.

"It was good seeing you, too." I replied, trying to keep my voice steady despite my racing heart. "Are you sure you can't at least share a few things, like am I going to have any of the Nelsons after me?"

Andre tilted his head and eyed me. "I can see why that's a concern."

"Rick Nelson was in here yesterday."

He straightened, returning his coffee cup to the counter, his brows wrinkled in concentration. "What did he want?"

I gulped, not expecting to be the center of his attention. It was kind of nice and overwhelming at the same time. "Honestly, I don't know. Maggie seemed to be the only one in the family who was pretty straightforward about her thoughts and opinions. I'm finding the rest of the family a bit too subtle. Actually, pretty sneaky."

Andre nodded; maybe he had experienced the same behavior. "Well, I can tell you that Renee flew into Charleston International Airport on Tuesday evening."

I narrowed my eyes. "She didn't waste any time. So she has an alibi, but why stop here and why the interest in the podcast?"

Andre glanced at me. "I can see how disturbing this can be. She said nothing threatening toward you, right?"

"No. She was a little too candid. It sounded like her family had been talking about the podcast. She said her father encouraged her to come, so maybe Maggie was still talking to her ex-husband. Or the podcast came up at a family gathering with her brother, Rick. I don't know. But it feels like something was said to shine attention on me and the podcast. It's clear to anyone that keeps up with social media that some suspicion has been shone on me about her death."

"Unfortunately." Andre picked up his coffee and sipped. He seemed to be thinking through my theory. "Sounds plausible about Renee. So she came over here to check out the person who could be a prime suspect. But she must not have seen anything in you that concerned her because she didn't confront you."

I made a face. "Can you really look at someone and tell that they're a killer?" I shook my head. "Not that I am."

Andre chuckled. "I figured that out for myself, Joss. I'm just concerned that you're safe." He rubbed his chin. "What about Rick? Any threats?"

"No, nothing like that. But it's possible he could rack up in real estate around here. I suppose he has an alibi too."

Andre chuckled again. "You're going to try to squeeze whatever you can out of me."

"Absolutely." I grinned, enjoying that he would consider talking to me. Our eyes met and while I knew he would have to go to work at some point, I didn't want him to leave. I could talk to him all day. Of course I had my own job to do. Like serve coffee.

The door chimes broke my heart. I had customers to take care of and as much as I didn't want to, I needed to get back to work.

My thoughts crashed further as I glimpsed Sammie and Blaze behind the detective.

My eyes connected with Blaze who had a sour look on his face.

Oh boy!

Tuesday, September 20, 9:40 a.m.

The look on my face must have alarmed Andre. He spun around to face Sammie and Blaze. I watched as both young men locked eyes with one another.

"Hey, Joss," Sammie said cheerfully as he approached the counter. He was oblivious to his grandson and the detective's stare down. "I heard you guys have a fresh batch of sweet potato pie today. You know I can't resist that."

I glanced at Blaze, before responding. "One slice coming right up, Mr. Sammie."

"Make that two," chimed Blaze, though his tone was markedly less enthusiastic than Sammie's. Instead of meeting my gaze, his eyes flicked nervously between Andre and me.

"Sure thing," I said. I grabbed two containers for the pies. Another reason why Blaze and I broke up was his mood swings. No doubt he was a great musician and DJ, but as quickly as he was the life of the party, he could also drag you down.

The other night, I knew he'd been upset about Sammie's memory issues, but today I could tell he just didn't like seeing me talking to another guy.

Probably didn't help that Andre was a cop.

I snapped the lid on the two generous slices of pie. "Here you go. Enjoy!"

"Thanks, Joss!" beamed Sammie, his eyes twinkled. It was good to see Sammie was in a better mood than his grandson.

Blaze paid for the order, barely managing a terse nod before turning to leave. He made a wide berth around Detective Baez as he followed Sammie to a table near the windows. I was grateful that Blaze sat with his back to me.

"Who is that?" asked Andre, his brow furrowed with concern. "He seems... tense."

I squirmed a bit before I answered. And though I was just answering Andre's question, I felt like a snitch. "Blaze. He's a DJ, and that's his grandfather Sammie Morrison."

Andre nodded. "You interviewed Mr. Morrison on the podcast."

"Yes, he was my grandfather's best friend. You've listened to all the episodes?" I forgot Blaze and his behavior as I focused on the detective. I knew it was his profession, but I appreciated that he remembered details.

Andre smiled. "I have."

That made me blush.

"And your relationship with Mr. Blaze?" he asked.

Too stunned to speak, I sputtered. "How did ..."

Andre finished his coffee before answering. "He's not over you."

I leaned closer, intrigued. "You can tell all of that from a brief encounter?"

"I'm a guy. It's not rocket science to know how another guy feels about a woman." Andre held up his cup. "Can I get a refill?"

"Sure." Fay had also warned me about being too close to my ex-boyfriend. But I wasn't so sure how I felt about Andre picking up on that. I definitely wanted him to know there was nothing going on.

I poured fresh coffee into his cup and handed it to Andre. "He's an ex. Nothing is going on."

Andre grinned. This time the exchange seemed even more intimate. I could barely tell the difference between the warmth of the cup and his fingers brushing mine.

"I'll see you around," he replied. "And if there is something I think you should know, I will tell you."

"Thanks, Detective." I watched him walk out of the café before taking the next order. After serving several orders, I grabbed a cloth to wipe tables. I wanted to know what was up with Blaze.

Sammie grinned as I approached, a crumb of pie clinging to the corner of his mouth. "This is good. Just the right amount of nutmeg and cinnamon."

"I know Fay will be happy to hear that." I turned to face Blaze. "Everything okay with you today?"

Blaze was busy tapping away on his smartphone, trying to appear nonchalant. But I could see the tension in his shoulders, the corners of his mouth drawn into a tight line.

"Blaze?" Annoyed, I put my hands on my hips. "What's your problem?"

He glanced up from his phone, his eyes narrowing as he met my gaze. "That cop sure hangs around you a lot," he replied curtly, his voice sharp and defensive.

I raised an eyebrow. "Not all cops are bad."

"Maybe," Blaze slipped his phone into his pocket and gave me his full attention. "But I've seen enough bad ones to be wary."

"Fair enough," I said, studying him more closely. He seemed exhausted, like he hadn't slept in a few days. I wondered how Sammie was doing. Was his memory issues getting worse? I had noticed that Sammie wasn't as talkative. In fact, he seemed more focused on the sweet potato pie and how it reminded him of his mama's pie.

"But you shouldn't judge someone just because of their profession. Besides, Detective Baez is doing his job."

Blaze huffed. "Why are you so friendly with him? Didn't he consider you a suspect in Maggie's murder last week?"

I bit my lip, feeling the heat rise in my cheeks. "I went to the station to make a statement. I'm sure if the other detective, Detective Wilkes wasn't there, it wouldn't have gone the way it did."

Blaze shook his head. "Well, I hope you don't regret trusting him."

Sammie spoke up. He appeared sobered now. "Cops aren't good. They didn't help your grandfather."

That punched me in the gut. What could I say?

"You're right, Mr. Sammie." I knew Blaze and Sammie meant well, but I liked Andre.

I believe he liked me, too.

"Look," I exhaled, feeling my frustration bubble up. "It's his job to ask questions and figure things out. That doesn't mean he wants to see me behind bars."

"Maybe," Blaze rubbed the back of his neck. "But they got to arrest someone eventually. Didn't you hear the radio this morning?"

I shook my head. It was a rough morning and I'd almost overslept. "No. What did I miss?"

"Rick Nelson put up a $50,000 reward. He wants to find his sister's killer. You're the one who found her. There's no way that detective doesn't have a motive for hanging around you."

Blaze might as well have slapped me. Not wanting to talk to him anymore, I spun around and headed back to the counter.

I knew Andre liked me. He wasn't the kind of guy who would play with my emotions. Of course, some men had fooled before me.

Did Andre have some other reason for showing interest in me?

Tuesday, September 20, 2:33 p.m.

Long after Blaze and Sammie left, my mind still reeled from Blaze's comment about Andre wanting to keep an eye on me as a potential suspect. The thought of it made my stomach churn like milk left out in the sun for too long. Why was it that as soon as I started liking a guy, the rug got pulled out from under me?

"Joss, you're doing that thing again," Fay said, appearing beside me with a knowing grin. "You know, where your face scrunches up like you've just bitten into a lemon?"

"Blaze mentioned something earlier, and I can't shake it." I told Fay what he said.

She raised an eyebrow. "Clearly the man is jealous. You used to date him. And I told you hanging out with him this past summer working on the podcast might not have been a good idea. Besides, Joss, if Detective Baez really thought you were a suspect, he'd be obligated to keep his distance, not get involved with you."

"We're not exactly dating," I pointed out.

"Not yet," Fay's grin widened.

I giggled. "I wouldn't mind if we were."

"Of course you wouldn't!" Fay laughed, patting me on the back. "Now don't let Blaze steal your joy." She frowned and crossed her arms over her chest. "You know Blaze is good at what he does, but I've never liked him for you. He's too intense."

"Yeah, but I wouldn't have been able to get this podcast done without him. His expertise means the world to me."

Fay looked at me. "I know. And I'm sure he's enjoyed the fact that you depended on him for that very reason."

I frowned. "You don't mind him being the DJ for Friday Night Jam."

Fay pointed a finger. "No. I went with him because he's your friend. Also, I'm fond of his grandfather. Sammie used to come out to the schools when I taught and teach the kids about jazz and bebop for a few weeks. I know how much Sammie loves his grandson, but everyone knows how much trouble Blaze used to get into."

"Yeah, but he's older now, and he takes care of his grandfather."

Fay threw up her hands. "You're right. But you gotta be careful when you are dealing with exes. There is always that one who wants things to be a certain way when you have moved on."

I appreciated Fay's advice. I wasn't sure if it made me feel any better though. On one hand, I wanted to get to know Andre better, but I considered Blaze a friend.

Chapter 16

Time to Fight Back

Wednesday, September 21, 9:57 p.m.

I didn't sleep that well last night. Getting a good night's sleep had been hit or miss for a few months now. First it was the excitement of getting the podcast edited. There were hours of audio, some of it not even making it to the final episodes that were now available everywhere. I'd fall into bed exhausted, but excited.

This past week I just hit the bed exhausted and almost depressed that all my hard work seemed to go down the drain. My mother had been right about the ramifications of creating the podcast.

That hurt even more.

I could feel the tension in the air when I entered the café on Wednesday. Fay was talking to Albertine Lancaster, the owner of the Book Nook, which was on the other side of the Crafty

Corner. They were in the back of the café comparing similar looking pieces of paper in their hands.

I frowned as I came through the swinging half-door. Hailey was working behind the counter today and her eyes were wide behind her glasses. I hurried to my locker and grabbed my apron.

I hissed at Hailey when I returned. "What's going on?"

Hailey looked at me and shook her head. "I don't know, but I've never seen Fay that mad before. She had all kinds of cuss words coming out of her mouth. I know my ears had to turn as red as they felt."

No, that's not good!

Fay wasn't one to lose her cool.

Not shy about being nosy, I walked up to Fay and Albertine. Albertine was a petite older Black woman, and a retired elementary school teacher. I loved walking into the bookstore when she was doing story time for the preschoolers. The most animated voices came out of her small frame. She'd asked me to come do story time for her and I told her I would once the podcast was published.

As I approached, I stopped to listen.

Fay's voice was tight with emotion, "I should have known when that man was in here on Monday, just a week after his sister was killed, that he was up to no good."

"He stopped by the Book Nook too. Picking up books and putting them back without even bothering to read the blurbs. He seemed more interested in assessing the value of the space than enjoying the atmosphere. Didn't even show a single bit of remorse when I expressed my condolences for Maggie," the bookstore owner, crossed her arms and shook her head.

"So what did he do?" My heart pounded in my chest.

Fay and Albertine turned to me. The anger in their eyes made me want to step back.

Fay pursed her lips before replying. "He's trying to get us to sell, wants to bring in some big-time development to this block."

I bit my lip, feeling a pang of worry for Sugar Creek Café. "No. He can't do that, right? He has to go to the city council and get approved."

Albertine sighed. Her shoulders sagging made her look even smaller. "He's probably going to get the approval he needs. Everyone on the council is in his back pocket."

Fay shook her head. "Not everybody. We might have a few allies, but we'll have to make the case with the others."

I frowned. "People come here because it's different. They're looking for a unique experience, not some cookie-cutter franchise. Is he even rebuilding with your businesses in mind?"

Fay rolled her eyes. "Not even. This letter states they want to build some luxury hotel."

I placed my hands over my mouth. "He wants to just bulldoze over all the buildings. These are people's dreams."

"Exactly! Rick has no right to come in here and disrupt everything we've worked for," Fay declared. "These are more than just businesses – they're our homes, extensions of ourselves."

"Absolutely," agreed Albertine. "Getting that bookstore was something I wanted so much. I saved years of money, not to mention some of my retirement."

Poor Ms. Albertine looked as if she would cry at any moment. Fay put her arms around the woman.

"Maybe we can rally the community, get them to stand with us?" I suggested.

"Maybe," said Fay. "We need to be smart and strategic about this. We can't let Rick Nelson intimidate us or force us to abandon what we've built."

"No wonder he couldn't answer my question the other day about what he wanted to do with the Crafty Corner. He wants the whole block." I frowned. "Is that what you meant the other day about Maggie's death being even worse than we imagined? I know she wasn't likeable, but it sounded like she stood her ground and protected the properties around here."

Then I sucked in a breath. "Wait. Is he going to destroy the Lofts too?"

Fay and Albertine exchanged looks.

Fay responded, "I don't know. The historical society has invested a lot into that building. It should be protected."

I took a deep breath. "We need to gather as much information as possible about Rick's plans. Knowledge is power, right?"

Fay shook her head. "Yes, but he has the money."

I was so tired of the Nelsons.

Lord, there has to be a way to stop the craziness this family brought with them.

Wednesday, September 21, 9:57 p.m.

I sat down on my bed with my laptop, knowing I wouldn't be able to sleep. I cringed at the images on my screen of a middle-aged man that had become my opponent. It's weird how my family and the Nelsons still remain connected in some cruel way.

I clicked on his social media profiles, scrolling through photos of him posing next to shiny cars at his dealership. His captions were peppered with car puns and cheesy jokes.

He was destroying lives. Just like his father.

I moved on to the car dealership website, watching commercials featuring Rick himself. He had a certain charm and charisma that could easily draw people in. But I could tell it was all a game to him.

"Trust me, folks! Here at Nelson Autos, we'll steer you in the right direction!"

"Ugh, this man is sickening." I groaned, rubbing my temples.

I clicked off the website, not really sure what the plan was here.

Whatever was bothering me started with Maggie's daughter. Andre said she came to town last Tuesday evening. It sounded like she found out about her mother's death in the early morning hours in California. Did the police call her? Or was it her dad or uncle?

Either way, for a woman she supposedly didn't care for, Renee made it to South Carolina in record time.

She was the one who first warned me about her uncle. That meant she must have had a conversation with him. Someone in her family told her about the podcast because she knew how upset Maggie had been about it.

"Renee, why did you really visit the café that day?" I whispered to myself. I couldn't shake the feeling that there was more to her visit. With the letters Fay and the other business owners received today, the reason for her uncle's visit on Monday became pretty obvious.

I typed Renee Nelson's name into the search bar, hoping to find something. My phone buzzed next to me on the bed. I peered down to see an Instagram notification on my lock screen — another message from Rae Silva. My heart raced as I unlocked my phone, wondering what this mysterious person had to say now.

"Do you feel good about what you've done to Maggie? Have you avenged your grandfather?"

My fingers hovered above the screen, hesitating for a moment before I clicked the profile. This time, I responded with a direct message.

Who are you, and why do you keep accusing me of something I didn't do?

I stared at my phone, waiting for an answer, but none came. The profile's glaring privacy setting prevented me from seeing any information about Rae Silva beyond their name.

I threw my phone on my bed.

Since I was in a digging mood, I pulled up Google and typed "Rae Silva" into the search bar.

I clicked through several pages of search results, each one less relevant than the last. It was like searching for a needle in a haystack.

I hopped off the bed and paced. "There has to be something. This person is local, or they certainly know about me and my family history."

I went to wash my face and brush my teeth. I had intentions of heading to bed, but something still nagged at me.

I sat back down on the bed and grabbed my laptop. The IG notification distracted me and I hadn't finished my search for Renee. She didn't have a Facebook profile, and there wasn't an IG profile under her name. But there were a plethora of photos on Instagram under Salty Café and Books.

Renee had a whole life out there in Cali. She looked like a beach girl who liked to surf the waves. There were pictures of her coffee shop. At least that wasn't a lie. Maybe she really was looking for ideas from Sugar Creek café. Her coffee shop, with its nautical theme and seashells, had the perfect decor for a shop by the beach.

She also had a handsome man back home too. Blond and bronzed with vivid blue eyes. They were a stunning couple.

Then I looked closer. Were they both wearing wedding rings?

I clicked on the picture to read the caption.

Me and hubby catching some waves today.

That was her husband. You go, girl!

Renee had linked to her husband's IG, so I clicked because he was nice to look at.

When I entered his page, I gasped. It was like a bolt of lightning.

@mikesilva

Her husband's name was Mike Silva.

Renee introduced herself to me as a Nelson. I scrolled through more pictures and photos that tagged @saltycafeandbooks.

From what I could tell, Renee's legal name had to be Renee Silva.

"Is Rae Silva really Renee Nelson?" There had to be a connection. It was certainly possible that she didn't go by Renee at all. Rae could be short for Renee.

"Alright, Renee or Rae, I don't feel like playing games with you." I pulled up the Rae Silva profile.

With my fingers hovering above my phone's screen, I thought carefully about how to word my message. I didn't want to sound accusatory, but I also wanted to make it clear that I wanted answers.

"Hey, Renee," I began, deliberately using her real name to show that I had uncovered her secret. "I've been getting messages from 'Rae Silva' accusing me of having something to do with Maggie's death. We met the other day, and I thought you could tell I genuinely did nothing to your mother. You need to stop this or I'm going to show this to the cops."

As my thumb hovered over the send button, I hesitated for a moment, unsure if I was ready to dive headfirst into this confrontation.

Then I hit send.

I stared at my phone, willing it to light up with a notification. I grew sleepy, tired of waiting. Realizing I could have been wrong, I confirmed my alarm was set for seven o'clock and crawled under the covers.

By the time my heavy eyes had closed, I heard my phone buzz. The sound sent a jolt of adrenaline coursing through me. I reached up and grabbed the phone.

My fingers quickly tapped in my passcode, and I sat up in bed as I reached for the message.

I'm sorry. You won't hear from me again.

I swung my feet over the side of the bed. "What? You're being a coward, like your grandfather."

I started to type my thoughts when I noticed another notification from the @saltycafeandbooks account.

I paused for a moment, confused, but I clicked over to the new direct message.

Joss, this is Renee. I'm so sorry about those posts. Rae is my daughter. She showed me what she did. I promise she will be punished and she won't bother you again. Please don't report her to the police. She's just a kid.

Wow! I stared at the message.

I didn't see that one coming at all.

My fingers tapped rapidly against the screen of my phone as I composed a new message. This time, though, it wasn't for Renee or Rae.

Hey, Andre, guess what? I found Rae Silva.

And this time, when I put my phone up, I smiled. I was pretty sure that would get Detective Baez's attention.

Chapter 17

Past History

COLD JUSTICE PODCAST
Episode 5: The First Responder

Joss: Welcome back to the *Cold Justice Podcast*. Today, I have a special guest with me, Officer John Lyons, who was the first responder at the scene of August Manning's murder. Officer Lyons, thank you for joining me today.

Officer Lyons: Thank you for having me, Joss. It's been many years, but the events of that day still resonate with me.

Joss: Officer Lyons, as the first person to arrive at the scene, you witnessed the aftermath of August's murder. Can you walk us through what you encountered that day?

Officer Lyons: I knew August. Watched him play ball. <pauses> I can still feel the shock and disbelief when I saw his lifeless body lying on the ground. You know, at first I couldn't tell who it was. They'd beat him so badly. But then his marred features became familiar, and I knew who he was. I had to set aside my anger and do what I could to secure the area.

Joss: In the years following August's murder, those individuals responsible were let go without charges. Can you shed some light on why that happened?

Officer Lyons: <sigh> The circumstances were complicated. No one saw what happened. There were weeks of bullying and even a small confrontation a few hours before from the alleged perpetrators. But they knew what they were doing. They drug him to an empty alley. In fact, people knew to stay away from that alley. Even in the daylight there was always darkness over that area.

Joss: How did the lack of charges and August's murder impact the community, particularly those who knew him personally?

Officer Lyons: The community loved August. Everyone looked forward to seeing him hit home runs. He would take off running around those bases like he was a gazelle. He represented a ray of hope. A homegrown boy about to make something of himself. Everyone saw the heckling and the bullying, but what could we do? It's hard to fight against someone backed by so much power and influence. August did the right thing. He didn't cause no trouble. Instead, he smiled and ignored. Nothing was going to get him down. That made his death even harder to bear. The lack of justice intensified a lot of feelings of anger and pain.

Joss: As a police officer, how did August's murder and its aftermath shape your perspective on the role of law enforcement and the need for accountability?

Officer Lyons: You know, I was the only black police officer on the force. So I'd faced my own issues. August's tragic death and not being able to find justice for him still haunts me to this day. I wondered if things would have turned out different if someone had the courage to step forward as a witness.

Joss: Thank you for sharing your insights, Officer Lyons.

Thursday, September 22, 8:23 a.m.

Just as I guessed, Andre was in the line at the café. He was looking down at his phone but would occasionally glance at me as I took care of the customers in front of him. When he arrived at the counter, I smiled.

"You're starting to be a regular, Detective Baez. Let me guess, a black coffee. Although I think you should try a banana nut muffin. Unless you are worried about your diet."

He chuckled. "Sure, why not? A little sugar with my usual black coffee won't hurt."

I grinned and took care of his order.

"Sounds like you had a busy night sleuthing." He raised an eyebrow. "I thought I told you to be careful with that."

I handed him his coffee and then pulled a brown bag for the muffin. "I did. Just a regular night of surfing social media and Googling." I picked up a muffin with some tongs, stuffed the muffin inside the bag and neatly folded it over.

"So?" he asked.

I narrowed my eyes at him. "I have a feeling I did your job last night."

Andre sighed. "I had a few other leads I needed to work on first. It wasn't like I forgot."

"Mmm. Well, Rae Silva is the daughter of Renee Nelson Silva. Granddaughter to Maggie Nelson." I frowned. "I wonder if Maggie had any contact with her granddaughter. I don't think there was any love there either. Maybe Renee's bitterness rubbed off on her daughter."

Andre licked his lips, trying to absorb my news. "Actually, Renee doesn't go by Silva. The plane ticket was under Renee Nelson. But I have someone running a background check on her. She owns a coffee shop out in San Diego and it's under her maiden name, too."

"Maybe she started it before she got married. I didn't dig too deep. Not sure how long she's been married. But she sent me a direct message." I pulled it up so Andre could read.

Andre shook his head. "Wow, you really have your own investigation going." He placed his hand over his heart. "You don't trust me?"

I smirked. "Oh, I trust you. But I can't have someone in my DMs starting mess."

Andre chuckled again. "I hear you." He turned serious, his eyes so laser focused on me I had to catch my breath. "Just be careful. If you run into something strange, text me immediately. Next time, it might not be as simple as an angsty teen."

I waved goodbye to him. Once again feeling sorry to see him go. I was really getting used to him being around. I wished we weren't always meeting when we were both on the job.

Or talking about Maggie and the Nelsons.

Thursday, September 22, 3:20 p.m.

One thing about working in a coffee shop, there was always something to do. I glanced at the clock and decided it was time to prepare one last fresh pot of coffee for the day. We would close in about two hours. Thankfully, business had picked back up this week.

Eleanor had returned each day, back to her usual routine. Once the pot brewed, I swung over her way.

"Hey, Eleanor," I said, walking over to the booth with the steaming pot. "How's the writing going?"

Eleanor looked up from her laptop, startled. She blinked behind her round glasses before smiling. "It's going well. Thank you for asking."

"Mind if I top off your cup?" I asked, holding up the coffee pot.

"Please do," she replied, pushing her empty cup toward me.

As I filled her cup, I inquired. "Can I ask what your new book is about?"

Eleanor hesitated. "Well, it's a work in progress, so things might change, but... it's about an artist whose friend goes missing under mysterious circumstances."

"An artist, huh?" I mused. "That sounds intriguing. What inspired the idea?"

Eleanor hesitated, taking a sip of her coffee as if to stall for time. "Alright," she sighed. "I trust you to keep this between me and you. The artist in my book is loosely based on someone we both know. "

A sudden chill ran down my spine. "Wait a minute," I said. "Are you talking about Claude? Is he the inspiration for your character?"

Eleanor looked stricken as if she'd done a bad thing. "I can't say for certain, Joss. There might be some aspects of Claude in there."

I leaned in even more. "And the missing friend – is that based on someone real too? Someone close to Claude, perhaps?"

Eleanor replied, visibly uncomfortable. "There was a young woman, Rebecca Montgomery, who went missing three years ago. She and Claude were quite close, and many people speculated about their relationship. Some even believed he might have had something to do with her disappearance."

I'd really just met Claude two years ago when I started working at the café. This was information I wasn't aware of. I felt my heart skip a beat. "Would you mind sharing a bit more about Claude's missing friend? I'm really curious to know what happened."

"Alright," she sighed. "Rebecca was beautiful and known for creating stunning sculptures. She and Claude were close, and they both shared a passion for their craft."

Eleanor continued, her voice taking on a somber tone. "You would have liked Rebecca. She was an activist for various causes. In fact, she would have been happy to help Fay and the other business owners with this Rick Nelson matter. She didn't like big business rolling over little people."

"Sounds like she was a real gem. So what happened? Why would people be suspicious of Claude?"

Eleanor sighed. "Rebecca was volatile. She had a temper. No one really knows what the argument was about and Claude shuts down if you ask him. But it was enough to cause a riff in their friendship."

"So they had a falling out before she disappeared?"

Eleanor nodded. "The day before. She simply vanished without a trace. It devastated Claude. I believe he really loved her, but she didn't see him that way. To her, he was just a friend."

"Thank you for sharing that with me, Eleanor," I said.

Though in the back of mind, I kind of wish I hadn't asked. I really liked Claude. I didn't want to think there was an evil bone in that man's body.

I also realized I hadn't seen Claude since last week. I knew he was putting the finishing touches on my grandfather's portrait.

Might be time to drop by.

Thursday, September 22, 6:31 p.m.

"See you in the morning," I shouted to Fay. She waved good-bye as I headed out. Tomorrow night would be the Friday Night Jam, which I'd been looking forward to since last week. It was what everyone needed to lift their moods.

The day had been gloomy with overcast clouds, threatening rain. This time of year, the sun made its descent fast. In a few weeks, time would fall back, which I couldn't stand. Shorter days and longer nights affected my mood.

I climbed into my car and headed in the opposite direction of home. In a few minutes, I turned into the side parking lot of the Lofts, which were empty except for Claude's beat up Chevy truck.

I was still a bit upset about my earlier conversation with Eleanor. I'd always known there was something bothering Claude. As good-looking as he was, I rarely saw him dating. Women were always trying to be all over him, but he'd wiggle away from them. He spent a lot of time by himself in the studio and his friends seemed to mainly be me, Eleanor, Fay, and Sammie.

As soon as I stepped out of the car, I started shivering. The temperatures were in the high sixties and dropping fast. I hadn't checked the weather app on my phone, but I could smell rain approaching. Goosebumps formed on my arms, which bore short sleeves. I wished I'd grabbed the light jacket I kept in my locker at the café. I sprinted for the building, hoping Claude would answer the door quickly.

I reached the front door and hesitated. The door stood slightly ajar. I peered closer, there was something like a brick keeping the door from closing.

This wasn't good for security. I slid the brick out of the way and stepped inside. The door shut with a click behind me. I glanced over at the music studio and noticed a light in the back. I peeked through the window next to the door, but didn't see Blaze inside. His car wasn't outside either. Maybe he'd just forgotten to turn off the light.

During the summer, I'd been inside the Lofts later than this to work on the podcast with Blaze. But daylight remained until well after eight o'clock during the summer months. Today, the cloudy weather and seasonal change was making it seem later than it actually was and the interior of the Lofts felt eerily quiet. My anxiety flowed to the surface. I tried to ignore the sense of dread creeping up my spine as I made my way to the stairs leading to Claude's studio.

When I reached the top of the landing, I froze. Claude's door stood wide open. My chest tightened, and my palms grew sweaty.

What was going on?

Now I realized I shouldn't have barreled forward into the building. "Hello?" I called out tentatively as I stepped closer to Claude's doorway. "Claude, are you here?"

Nothing. I was glad I'd grabbed my phone from the car before I got out. Thankfully, I had a habit of always having it in my hand. I looked down at the screen, thinking of Detective Baez's earlier warning.

Just be careful. If you run into something strange, text me immediately.

I peered around, ready to flee back down the stairs. But like over a week ago when faced with entering the Crafty Corner, I knew something wasn't right. Claude would not leave his door wide open. The man had all kinds of locks on the door to protect his studio.

I quickly texted Andre.

Something's off at the Lofts. Please help.

I cringed at how Andre might react to my text, but I needed to know if Claude was okay. When he was in the throes of painting, he wouldn't leave the studio, even choosing to use food delivery. I assumed that's why he hadn't been at the café lately.

I stepped up to the open door. "Claude, are you in here?" I sucked in a breath. The studio was a mess. My heart raced. I fought the urge to run again, but took a deep breath and continued further inside.

Canvases were strewn about, paint splatters marred the floor, and a broken easel leaned against the wall. Amongst the chaos, I spotted my grandfather's portrait lying on the ground. My breath hitched, and I clutched my chest in a mixture of fear ... and anger.

"Claude?" I called out again, my voice wavering slightly. "Where are you?"

Suddenly, my gaze fell upon a crumpled figure lying motionless on the floor. "Oh, no." I raced over to him.

"Claude!" I gasped, kneeling down beside him. His face was pale, and his eyes were closed. There was a bruise forming on his temple, and a trail of blood down his mouth. It looked like someone had beaten him up pretty badly.

Had this been a robbery?

"Come on, Claude, wake up," I urged, shaking his shoulders to rouse him. "Who did this to you?"

My heart pounded in my ears as I grabbed my phone to dial 911. But before I could press the buttons, a noise startled me from behind and I spun around.

A dark figure stood in the doorway and I started screaming.

Chapter 18

The Betrayal

Thursday, September 22, 7:01 p.m.

The figure stepped forward and held out his hands. "It's okay, Joss. It's just me. I was working in the studio and brought Pops with me so I could keep an eye on him. I thought maybe he'd come up here to see Claude. I can't find him." Blaze moved forward into Claude's studio. "What happened?"

My ears were still ringing from my screams. "I don't know. I need to dial 911."

"I can do that." Blaze said.

"Okay." I croaked. I looked back at Claude, still confused at who would do this to him and why.

Lord, help. I don't know what's going on.

I turned to see if Blaze had dialed 911, but he was looking at me with a forced smile on his face. What alarmed me more, despite the dim lighting, I could tell his clothes looked disheveled. I peered down at his hand, which clutched his phone.

Was that bruising on his knuckles?

Had he been in a fight?

But why? And, with who?

Before I could ask the questions charging through my mind, I heard Claude stirring beside me, his eyes opening and closing.

"Claude." I reached for his hand. "You're awake. We're going to get some help."

Claude looked at me, dazed. "Joss, how did you get in here?"

"Someone propped the entrance to the building open. Your door was open too. What happened in here?"

"I..." Suddenly, Claude clutched my hand, his gaze going over my shoulders. "Joss, be careful!"

My eyes darted between Claude and Blaze.

"Blaze?" I said, trying to sound calm despite my growing suspicions. "Did you call 911 yet?" I remembered Blaze telling me about Sammie wandering off one time and getting lost. It explained why he was staying so close to him. "If Sammie is missing, we need to get help to find him too. It's going to start raining soon."

I was babbling, but in the back of my mind, I knew that something had gone very wrong.

Blaze didn't respond and avoided eye contact with me. Instead, he and Claude seemed to be locked into a staring match.

"Blaze?" I prompted. "What's going on?"

Blaze finally looked into my eyes. "Joss, please," he pleaded. "I had to do something."

I barely recognized my strangled voice. "What did you do?"

Blaze opened his mouth, hesitating before speaking again. "I didn't want to hurt Claude. But I couldn't let him go to the police."

I returned my attention to Claude, who'd been trying to sit up. "The police. For what?"

"You know how important Pops is to me." Blaze began shifting uncomfortably on his feet.

"Of course, I know how much Sammie means to you."

Blaze wasn't making sense. He could be hot-headed and had constantly gotten into trouble when he was younger. I knew this wasn't the first time he'd assaulted a man.

"August?"

We all turned to find Sammie had entered the room. His hands reached out in front of him as he shuffled over to the painting of my grandfather on the floor.

"August." Sammie cried. "I'm so sorry."

My confusion whirled. I was still trying to process what happened between Blaze and Claude, and now Sammie was here. Where had he gone? At least he was safe and we didn't have to send out a search party.

Blaze's face moved from horror to fear. "Pops, where did you go? I went looking for you!"

I frowned. Sammie definitely didn't appear like his mind was in the present.

"August..." Sammie wailed, his hand trembled as he touched the canvas. Tears had welled up in his eyes, spilling over and streaking down his weathered cheeks. "I should've stopped them. Chuck and his buddies, they just kept hitting you. I was there, watching from a distance, wondering if I should get help."

I gulped, a bit horrified at what I'd just heard.

Sammie had been there that day.

He'd been the witness my grandfather's case needed.

"Take it easy, Pops," Blaze said. "You couldn't have known things would turn out the way it did. There was nothing you could do about it."

"I could see you weren't moving anymore, August." Sammie continued. "I did nothing to help you. Chuck Nelson has always been a bully, trying to make us feel small. Like we weren't men."

Sammie's voice took on a steelier tone. "August, I couldn't help you, but I protected your baby girl."

Air entered my lungs in a whoosh. I hadn't realized that my breath had grown shallow, frozen in the revelation of Sammie's admission of being a witness.

Then what he'd said hit me.

Protect. Baby Girl.

Sammie was in the café when Maggie came in harassing me about the podcast.

Did Sammie confront Maggie?

"Blaze, what is he saying? What does he mean?"

Blaze cast me a concerned glance. "Pops is clearly not in his right state of mind."

I glanced from Sammie's tear-streaked face to Blaze, my mind a whirlwind of emotions. But Sammie had just confessed. Had that secret been gnawing at him for over six decades? When I interviewed him, and when others talked to him over the years, Sammie's story had always been the same. That he'd left and walked home. But now he was saying he had been close by and witnessed the whole thing.

And it sounded like he'd confessed to something else a lot more recent. Why else would Blaze assault Claude? All the fear about the police became even more obvious.

I crossed my arms over my chest, feeling a chill move up and down my upper body. "You both showed up at the café that night? Had you gone to see Maggie?"

Blaze sighed, running a hand over his head. "Pop was supposed to be waiting outside the café. I told him I would pick him up and bring him home. Instead, I heard him yelling. He was inside her shop, but he never laid a hand on her. I saw the whole thing. She got scared, tripped, and fell backwards." Blaze shook his head. "Her head hit the corner of a shelf, I guess. I pulled Pops out of there and took him to the studio so I could figure out what to do."

My mind flashed back to when I'd discovered Maggie's lifeless body, and the pieces clicked into place. I remembered the positioning of the shelf near her head.

Blaze continued, "I knew we needed to call somebody, but I knew Maggie would rain down fire on Pops. I didn't realize she'd hit her head that hard. We were on our way back when Pops saw you running out of Maggie's shop. You look so scared. Pops insisted that we stop to check on you." He held up his hand. "Pops was just trying to protect you. He didn't go in there to hurt her. Just to tell her to stop messing with you."

I looked over at Sammie. The weight of what he did recently and his guilt from all the years before seemed to lie on his bent shoulders. Sammie looked utterly defeated as he stared at my grandfather's portrait.

"Joss," Blaze pleaded, "it was an accident. Turning Pops in won't bring Maggie back."

I threw up my hands. "So what was the plan with beating up Claude? You just got yourself into more trouble. Who's going to look after Sammie now?"

Blaze's face fell. "I reacted without thinking."

I turned to Claude who'd sat himself upright leaning against the cabinet that held his paints. "How did you find out?"

Claude looked at me. "Sammie practically told me when I went over to play chess with him earlier this week. He was in such a state about Maggie, and it had been eating at me all week. I don't know if you realized how steamed he was when Maggie came into the café. It was like he saw what happened to August all over again."

Claude rubbed his head. "I went out for some food and saw Blaze coming out of his studio. I asked him to come up, told him we needed to get the cops off your back and that they would probably go easy on Sammie. Dude went berserk on me. We fought and, as you can see, my studio is ruined."

I frowned and stared at Blaze.

"I'm sorry. I just knew what Pops was going through. I can't see him behind bars. Not at his age. His mind isn't right." Blaze held up his hands. "I would never let you take the blame, Joss."

The sound of footsteps outside caught our attention. We all froze, our eyes darting toward the entrance.

Detective Andre Baez stepped inside, gun drawn and ready. His gaze met mine. "Joss, are you okay?"

"Y-yes," I replied hesitantly.

He lowered his gun slightly, but I could see the tension in his muscles, the readiness to react at a moment's notice. "What's going on?"

I glanced at Blaze, who'd shifted uneasily. Then he reached inside his jacket. Panic seized me, fearing the worst.

"Don't!" I shouted.

Thursday, September 22, 7:37 p.m.

"Show me your hands!" Detective Baez's voice boomed as he took a stance, pointing his gun directly at Blaze.

Blaze glanced over at me with wide eyes. He'd already assaulted Claude and had been covering up Sammie's involvement in Maggie's death. What was he planning to do with a cop here?

"Please, Blaze," I hissed. "Put it down. Sammie needs you."

Blaze's eyes shifted to Sammie, who now looked at his grandson.

Sammie shook his head. "Son, what are you doing?"

Blaze hesitated, his breaths shallow and strained. He slowly raised his hands in the air. "I just wanted you to know I was carrying."

"Okay." Andre held his gun on Blaze. "Put the weapon down nice and easy."

Slowly, Blaze pulled the gun out of his jacket and laid it on the floor. Then, he returned his hands in the air.

I breathed a shaky sigh, but it wasn't relief I felt. Blaze and Sammie were in so much trouble it made my stomach twist in knots.

"Kick it toward me." Detective Baez demanded. I watched as Blaze nudged the gun across the floor with a swift kick, sending it skidding toward the detective.

As if on cue, several uniformed officers came through the door. They quickly surrounded Blaze, grabbing his arms. As handcuffs were snapped around his wrists, the sharp metallic clicks echoed in my ears, making tears sting my eyes.

I knew from being around Blaze that he carried a gun on him. This could have escalated badly if Andre had shot him. Or vice versa.

"Are you okay, Joss?" Detective Baez stepped forward, his eyes filled with concern.

"Y-yeah, I'm fine," I stammered, trying to sound more composed than I felt. "You brought the calvary."

He gave me a brief head nod. "Your text, along with an alert from the security company, helped with that decision."

My eyes widened. "Right. The door was propped open."

Andre stared at me. "And you entered anyway?"

I wasn't the only impulsive one tonight. I held my head down. "I know. It was stupid. I should have learned my lesson from last week."

"Someone's looking out for you." Andre commented.

Thank you, Lord!

Andre stepped around me to where Claude sat on the ground. "We will get you to the hospital shortly, okay?"

Claude grimaced. "Thank you."

Detective Baez put his phone to his ear, eyeing me like he didn't quite know what to do with me.

I didn't blame him. I probably appeared to be a whole lot of trouble.

I went to stand by Claude. "I'm sorry about the studio."

Claude shrugged and then grimaced. "It probably wasn't smart of me to confront Blaze about what I heard Sammie say. I love Sammie too. I didn't want to go to the cops either, but I told Blaze that you didn't deserve to get all this bad attention from folks. I've seen what people have been saying about you and the podcast on social media."

"Thanks," I whispered. Now I felt guilty for thinking Claude had something to do with Maggie's death.

My gaze darted back to Detective Baez, who'd gone over to talk quietly to Sammie. A few minutes later, my heart broke when officers took Sammie away. I noticed they didn't handcuff him.

The paramedics arrived and weaved their way through the mess in the studio toward Claude. His face had swollen considerably, and he appeared to be holding his arm close to his body.

I followed the paramedics down the stairs and watched them load the gurney carrying Claude into the ambulance. Andre came up behind me. "We should get you home."

"My car is over there. I can drive. It's not that far."

"Are you sure?" His warm eyes, now very familiar to me, comforted me a bit.

He did what he said he would do. Come when I needed him. I just hoped I hadn't blown any chances of us getting to know each other outside of all of this tonight.

I bit my lip to keep my tears back. "Can you please make sure Sammie is okay? He's... he's been through a lot. And Blaze said he might have dementia or Alzheimer's."

A pained look crossed Detective Baez's face when he looked over at the patrol car where Sammie sat in the backseat. "That's a shame. Yeah, I'll look out for him." He eyed me. "You should go. Rain is coming soon. I will need you to make a statement."

"I hope I don't have to deal with Detective Wilkes again."

Andre held my gaze. "I will make sure that you don't have to."

"Okay." That was some relief.

I climbed into my car, but it took me a minute to start the engine. Next to my car, Blaze's Charger had been haphazardly parked like he was in a hurry. He must have been frantic trying to find Sammie. I held my face in my hands.

Why did he have to assault Claude? Poor Sammie!

My body felt numb as I sat watching big droplets of rain hit the windshield. Shock at tonight's events overwhelmed me, and I started shaking from more than just the chilly air.

By the time I drove off with the Lofts in my rearview mirror, tears poured down my face, soaking my shirt.

Friday, September 23, 10:04 a.m.

In a rare move, Fay closed the café on Friday and postponed Friday Night Jam.

Again.

With Blaze booked into custody and sitting in jail, we were without a DJ. Word spread fast about the police presence at the Lofts last night. When I got home, after filling in my grandmother, I called Fay, who I knew would be pretty upset about Sammie.

We were all so fond of him.

The next morning, since Fay closed the café, I headed straight to the hospital. The attending ER doctor kept Claude overnight to make sure he didn't have a concussion.

Thankfully, his arm wasn't broken, but he had a small fracture in his elbow from his fall. Claude's slim frame was no match for Blaze's muscles.

"So are they letting you out of here soon?" I asked.

Claude nodded. "Yeah, I should be released by lunchtime. Just waiting for one final evaluation from the doctor."

I shook my head. "I don't know what Blaze was thinking."

Claude sighed. "Like I said last night, I went about it the wrong way, I guess. I shouldn't have insisted that he go to the police. Of course, he wasn't going to turn in his grandfather."

I frowned. "How did the studio get so messed up?"

"I guess Blaze just had some pent-up emotions and I was the last straw. He didn't touch me at first, he just started knocking stuff off my table. That's when I threw myself at him, trying to make him stop."

Claude touched his bruised jaw. "He threw a left hook that sent me flailing back into my canvas. Next thing I knew, I was on the floor and he just kept going. I tried fighting back, but after a while the room blurred and I guess I lost consciousness."

I bit my lip. "Violence is never the answer." I was really disappointed in Blaze. All summer he'd worked with me on the podcast and he knew how violence ended for my grandfather. It was what split us up as a couple too. Even if Blaze was trying to protect Sammie, there had to be a better way.

"Mr. McKnight, how are you feeling this morning?"

I turned around to see Andre had entered the room. My body tensed at the sight of him. I knew I must have looked like a wreck while he came strolling in off the pages of *GQ* magazine.

Claude shrugged. "Feels like I've been run over by a car or something." He peered up at the detective. "Is Sammie okay?"

Andre nodded. "Sammie is in good care. He's not in a jail cell like his grandson. We thought it would be better to get him evaluated. Depending on his diagnosis, it will be up to the D.A. if he presses charges for Maggie's death. If his condition is confirmed, maybe there's a chance for leniency."

I frowned. "Maggie's brother is probably going to insert some pressure, but you all can prove it was an accident, right?"

Andre blew out a breath. "Yes, we can probably lay out the scenario based on Blaze's recollection. He's not the most reputable witness right now though. And I'm pretty sure Rick Nelson will have his say about the matter."

A doctor came in, followed by a nurse to check on Claude.

I followed Andre out of the hospital room. "Can I ask if there is evidence that will influence the D.A. to charge Sammie?"

"Forensics had narrowed down some DNA evidence," he explained. "We matched it up to the people you mentioned were there when Maggie had her outburst at the café. Blaze actually came up as a familial match since he has a record. With further investigation, we concluded it could have been Sammie. I was going to bring him in to talk to him before everything went awry last night at the Lofts."

"Thanks for telling me," I murmured.

"Joss," Andre began, his voice hesitant. "Why were you there last night?"

I looked at him, feeling sheepish. "I... I almost thought it was Claude," I admitted. "Something Eleanor, the author who's always at the café, said. She'd mentioned that Claude had been in trouble with the police before. And I knew that Claude and Maggie had a huge disagreement."

Andre sighed, rubbing the back of his neck. "That would have been dangerous if it was him. You know you can't go confronting suspects on your own like that," he chided.

I nodded. "I never wanted it to be someone I knew. It was an accident. The D.A. has to keep that in mind too. Sammie is such a good person, despite everything. I never knew that he witnessed my grandfather getting assaulted. He always mentioned that he'd left August and how he wished he'd stayed with him."

Detective Baez's expression softened. "I know that's hard to swallow. I'm sure Sammie was scared and wanted to do something. But back in those days he wouldn't have stood a chance even if he'd come forward. In fact, Sammie might not be here today himself."

I closed my eyes, trying not to think about it. It was the past. Sammie had clearly been suffering all these years, probably feeling the pain now as his memories slipped away from him.

I opened my eyes and caught Andre's warm brown eyes watching me. I couldn't help but feel that spark of connection between us.

"By the way," I said, "I didn't have time to thank you for coming when I sent you that text. I know it was pretty vague."

"Thank you for trusting me. I know it was hard on you when you came to the station last week." He responded, his gaze never leaving mine. "You have good instincts, but I want you to promise me you will be careful in the future."

I held up my hand like I was taking an oath. "I promise."

He chuckled. "Something tells me that Joss Miller is just getting started."

I wasn't about to disagree with him. I wasn't sure what would happen with the podcast now that I might not have Blaze's help. I just knew podcasting would not be a one-time gig for me like most things had been in my life.

Epilogue
Friday Night Jam

Friday, October 14 at 7:30 p.m.

The air inside Sugar Creek Café buzzed with anticipation for Friday Night Jam. Locals eager for a night of music sat at tables or stood shoulder-to-shoulder near the stage in the back of the café. The scent of freshly brewed coffee mingled with wafts of sweet, buttery pastries.

The hum of conversation and laughter filled the air until the lights dimmed, signaling the start of the show. When DJ Nyla B took the stage, the noise level rose.

"Hey, Sugar Creek!" she shouted into the microphone, her voice filled with excitement. "Are you ready to jam?"

The crowd erupted into cheers, and I couldn't help but clap along with them. Nyla's presence was infectious, and I was so thrilled she'd accepted the invitation.

I still missed Blaze though. Despite his impulsive nature, he was a beast behind the turntable and knew how to have a good time. He'd been charged with the assault on Claude. Against everyone's wishes I went to see him and passed along the business card for the attorney, Charles Barnaby. Thanks to the attorney and Blaze pleading guilty, they were able to work out a plea deal that reduced the assault charges down to a misdemeanor. There was still some jail time for less than a year, and then he'd be on probation. The hope was that Blaze would be back for Sammie who'd been provided around the clock care at a nursing home.

"Alright, let's get this party started!" Nyla B declared, flipping a switch on her DJ booth. The room instantly filled with the pulsating beats of a classic hip-hop beat. Nyla B skillfully mixed tracks, blending one song into the next.

"Go Nyla! Go Nyla!" I rocked to the rhythms, feeling good for the first time in several weeks. I looked to my right and saw Claude rocking to the beat too.

I nudged him with my elbow. "You look like you're feeling better."

"Better every day, Joss," he replied. Thankfully his fight with Blaze resulted in minor injuries. Claude had been determined to get his studio back in order, which I helped him do.

I glanced over at the café wall where my grandfather's portrait hung. "I really appreciate you working on the portrait. I hope you didn't overdo your arm."

Claude waved his hand. "It wasn't too damaged and I was almost finished. Plus, I felt like the painting had become a symbol of healing."

I smiled. "Thank you. A lot has happened. I'm thankful the D.A. showed some mercy to Sammie. That nursing home appears to be able to meet his needs. I'm just so sorry as he loses his memories that some of the sad ones are still there haunting him."

Claude looked at me. "You're not upset? Sammie saw everything. What if he had come forward or even went to get help?"

I bent my head. I'd thought about the fact that all these years Sammie had been the witness Officer Lyons mentioned they needed. I shook my head. "It still would have been difficult back then to get justice. And who knows, Sammie may not have lived this long either if he had intervened."

Fay came over, smiling for a change. It was good to see her in a good mood. Rick Nelson didn't win the approval of the city council for his development project, but word had gotten around that he would return and try again.

"Joss, do you see who's here?" Fay asked. "Why didn't you tell me?"

"Who? What are you talking about?" I scanned the room. Then I spotted someone — that made me stop in my tracks.

Actually, two people.

Detective Andre Baez had appeared out of nowhere. He leaned against the wall chatting with my anti-social mother, like they'd known each other for years.

"How does my mom know Andre?" I asked.

Fay shrugged. "I pointed him out to her. She wanted to know who he was. Sounds like Louise had been talking about him."

I groaned. If it wasn't my grandmother in my ear about Andre, it was Leesa. Never had I ever had this many people so interested in me getting to know a guy. Most of the time, people were telling me to make better choices and stay away from the guys I ended up liking.

Fay nudged. "Girl, if Detective Baez has your mom's approval, you have no excuses. Go on over there and see what's up."

I sighed. My mother never liked a single guy I dated. In fact, she was pretty vocal the entire time I dated Blaze. I was really surprised she hadn't been chirping 'I told you so' in my ear after how things went down last month.

As I approached, Andre caught my eye. Although he was talking to my mother, he held my gaze.

He had a way of looking at me that started my heart pounding in my chest. With the tight white shirt I wore, I wouldn't be surprised if people could see my heart leaping on my chest like on one of those cartoons.

"Hey, Joss," he greeted me with a warm smile.

"Detective." I turned to my mother. "Mom. You never come to Friday Night Jam."

She shrugged. "You're always talking about it and posting on social media. Plus, it was time for me to see this portrait that Aunt Thelma, Aunt Ruth, and Louise have been talking about."

I grinned and turned to stand next to her. "Do you like it?"

My mother wasn't much for affection, so it surprised me when she reached out to hug me.

She looked at me and then at the portrait. "I'm so proud of you, Joss. Thank you for honoring my dad like this."

"Of course." I stuttered, feeling suddenly flustered. This was so unexpected that I felt tears threatening my lashes.

My mother shook her head as if to rid herself of the brief show of emotions. She faced me. "So, I hear you have been doing the detective's job."

Still a bit shaky from my mom's display of vulnerability, I found myself with no words. I glanced at Andre.

He leaned forward. "Your daughter has a knack for investigating, but she should probably leave some of it to the professionals."

My mother eyed me. "I'm glad she has someone who can keep her straight. I'm going to leave you two to talk."

"Okay." I watched my mother walk to the other side of the room. It was good to see her out and enjoying herself for a change.

"How are you, Joss?"

I tilted my head up toward the familiar voice. Andre had drawn closer to me when my mom walked away, leaving barely a few inches between us. The scent of his aftershave wafted over me.

I gulped before responding. "I'm still trying to adjust to what's happened."

"That's understandable. You were close to Sammie and Blaze." He inquired. "Are you going to keep doing the podcast?"

I nodded. "Probably. But I'm going to take a break for a while. Wait for the right case." I looked up at him expectantly. "Maybe you have some suggestions."

He chuckled. "Oh no. I don't have any suggestions." Andre paused and looked thoughtful. "Well, maybe I do have something in mind."

I clasped my hands together. "You have a case?"

"Not that kind of suggestion. I was thinking more like asking you to grab dinner sometime." Then he added, "I would like to get to know you better."

For a moment, with my brain struggling to process what he said, all I could do was stare at him. While I could hear Nyla B playing music in the background, my focus was solely on the man who'd walked into the café over a month ago. From that very moment, there was something about him that captured my attention.

And he wanted to get to know me better.

I grinned up at him, pretty sure I looked way too eager. But I didn't care. "Dinner sounds great."

"Good. Since I already have your number, I'll call you to set something up soon."

"I'm going to hold you to that, Detective Baez."

"Andre." He prompted.

My heart fluttered open with the possibilities, like a flower in bloom. I was certainly looking forward to getting to know Andre Baez, the man.

Author's Note

In the past decade or more of writing book series, I have on more than one occasion had a minor character become a main character in a spin-off series. Jocelyn "Joss" Miller was first introduced in **Oven Baked Secrets**, the second book in the Eugeena Patterson Mysteries.

Joss displayed a natural curiosity and investigative spirit that led her to find her biological grandmother, Louise Hopkins. I always thought Joss would want to dive more into her family's history, to learn more about her biological grandfather, August Manning and his untimely death.

One of the quirks of writing a cozy mystery, often the town or community or even a particular place stands out as a "character" too. I have had just as much fun creating the Sugar Creek Neighborhood as I have developing each character in this community.

Most neighborhoods have a local coffee shop, which I briefly introduced in a *Lemon Filled Disaster*, book three of the Eugeena Patterson Mysteries. By the time I'd finished writing *A Simmering Dilemma*, book four of the Eugeena Patterson Mysteries, I knew I wanted to pursue a separate storyline for Sugar Creek Café and its budding amateur sleuth and barista. I also loved the idea of bringing in familiar characters like Eugeena Patterson-Jones, Amos Jones, Leesa Patterson and many more from the Sugar Creek community.

Ideas for the Joss Miller Mysteries started in 2020, but it wasn't until late 2022, that the idea formed to make Joss a podcaster. That new addition to the plot provided a whole new set of ideas for this character and stretched me in a different direction creatively.

I hope you enjoyed the first book in the series. Joss is already working on an investigation for the next season of *Cold Justice Podcast*. And there will be a lot more to the budding romance between Joss and Detective Andre Baez.

A Latte Mayhem

After the success of her first true crime podcast series, barista Joss Miller returns with a new season of the *Cold Justice Podcast*. Joss dives into the investigation of local artist and activist, Rebecca Montgomery, who went missing three years ago.

As Joss pieces together the puzzle, someone is determined to keep the truth buried. Now six months into dating Detective Andre Baez, Joss's determination to find the truth could jeopardize their relationship and her life.

Chapter 1

Stirring Mayhem

Wednesday, April 15 at 10:05 a.m.

There's only been a few times in my life when I've felt my body floating, even though I was standing still. I could hear the murmur of conversations around me. Even the mixed scents of freshly brewed coffee and sweet cinnamon rolls didn't break my focus.

Really it was only a few seconds, but the longer I laid my eyes on the man in front of me, the warmer my body felt.

"Okay, I would normally say, you two need to get a room, but Ms. Joss Miller here is working. Detective Baez, don't you have some case to solve?"

I tore my eyes away from the detective, my cheeks now warm from embarrassment and looked at my boss. "Um, I was giving Detective Baez his order." I snuck a glance at him. "He's such a faithful customer."

Fay crossed her arms, she eyed me and then Detective Baez. "Really, Joss." She shook her head before heading to the back of Sugar Creek Café.

Detective Andre Baez came into the café every morning like clockwork. I told him he was a café resident now. We had several patrons who visited daily. While he loved our special blend of coffee, he was also my boyfriend.

Boyfriend.

I often wanted to pinch myself. We'd been dating for almost six months. And I was very much in love.

The way Andre gave me his full attention, I felt pretty sure he was smitten with me too.

He grinned. "Sorry. I didn't mean to get you into trouble."

I waved my hand. "It's fine. Fay's been in a mood the past few days. I don't know if you heard, but the Davis family down the street are closing their boutique. They're on the other side of the Book Nook. So there will be two empty storefronts on this block."

Andre let out a slow whistle. "Really, that's got to be tough. I thought everyone was united in not selling."

I shrugged. "That's what I thought, but apparently Rick Nelson worked his magic. Plus, Mrs. Davis is up in age and she's been trying to get one of her children to take over the shop for years. I think she's just tired. Money looked good towards her retirement."

This all started late last year when the owner of the craft store next door, Crafty Corner, was killed. There had been quite a bit of fallout from Maggie Nelson's death. One of them being her younger brother, Rick Nelson, inheriting the property. He decided to shut down the craft shop. For the past six months, he's been focused on a campaign that would bring in developers. The primary goal – to build a luxury hotel.

It would only be a matter of time before Rick Nelson started hounding Fay about selling the café again. He sent a letter late last year, which both Fay and her fellow business owner, Albertine Lancaster of the Book Nook verbally protested at a city council meeting. Fay was pretty popular on social media and brought her grievances to her followers, who flooded Nelson online with posts.

However Rick tried to come at Fay, he would have to tread carefully.

I knew how much Fay loved this place. The café had been like home to me. Fay had been really good to me. Not only as a mentor, but she'd been like a big sister to me. When I struggled a few years ago to find my way, she gave me a chance. I'd always like coffee, but being a barista hadn't really crossed my mind. Now I was Fay's right hand woman, the assistant manager of Sugar Creek Café.

"Tell Fay it will be okay. The café has quite the fanbase, and Rick Nelson doesn't ." Andre's cell phone beeped from his pocket.

I watched as he reached for the phone hooked to his belt. His eyebrows creased as he read the message. He reached for his coffee cup. "I need to go."

"Do you want a refill?" I hoped he would hint at what had made his handsome face worried.

He shook his head. "Thanks, I'm good. I'll see you tonight."

"Okay." My mood dropped a bit as he headed out. The familiar door chimes rang. I wondered where he was going and if it was a new case. I looked around Sugar Creek Café taking in the cozy atmosphere. The thought of losing all this to some soulless redevelopment project sent a chill down my spine.

I walked in the back to check on Fay. I found her at her desk, staring at the laptop. "Are you okay?"

Fay sighed. "Yeah. I'm sorry. I'm glad you two are still going strong."

"Me too." I hadn't had the best track record with dating and had taken long extended man fasts in between.

"Have you talked to Mrs. Davis? Any chance she might change her mind."

"Unfortunately, no." Fay frowned. "She said that Rick offered her more money than she could ever imagined, but I felt like there was something else she wasn't telling me."

"Like what? Do you think he tried to intimidate her?"

Fay sighed. "I wouldn't put it past Rick Nelson. You know more than most that the whole family is a bunch of bullies."

Yes, I knew that well. The Nelsons and I had crossed paths too many times for me to care.

I asked a question that I already knew the answer to. "Do you think Rick Nelson is coming to pressure you?"

Fay smirked. "I have no doubts that he will try. He's probably going to leave me for last. I just hope other business owners don't cave to him. I don't want us to be left standing alone."

I heard the chimes of the café door indicating a customer had arrived or left. "Hang in there. Let me go out and take care of this customer."

As my gaze swept the customer at the counter, my heart broke a little as I spotted Claude McKnight. A very talented artist, the café practically was a gallery of sorts featuring all kinds of artwork by Claude. One of my favorite pieces was one I commissioned him to do for me.

A large portrait of my grandfather August Manning. A charismatic young man from this community, whose life was cut short years ago, was now seen by the many people that graced our doors.

As I approached the counter, I put on a smile to hide my concern. Claude was a handsome man, but he always looked like a starving artist. Today, he appeared more disheveled than usual, his dirty blonde hair unkempt and dark circles under his eyes.

"Hey, Claude," I greeted him. "What can I get you?"

He gave me a small smile. "I'll take an espresso and one of those banana nut muffins."

"Sure thing." After he swiped his card, I said, "I'll bring it out to you."

"Great." He turned to look around the café. "I'm going to talk to Eleanor."

Eleanor Olsen was one of our regular residents and a local mystery author. She often acted as a surrogate mother to Claude, and he a surrogate son.

I added Claude's order to a tray and walked it over to the table. "How's it going, you two?"

Eleanor smiled. "It's been a good morning. Especially now since I get to see two of my favorite people."

I grinned. "I appreciate you, Eleanor."

I placed the tray in front of Claude. "Is everything okay?"

He took a sip of the espresso and sat for a few seconds, almost like he needed the liquid to boost his energy before responding. "It's been hard these past few days."

His eyes darted around nervously as if he was afraid someone might overhear. "I know I can share this with you two," he admitted. "You know about my friend Rebecca Montgomery, right?"

I nodded. "Yes, she went missing almost three years ago now."

Eleanor asked, "Has there been any breaks in her case?"

Claude crossed his arms and then uncrossed them and placed his hands on the table. "Her birthday was Saturday and her sister came to visit me at the studio. She asked me all kinds of questions. The same ones she asked me last year and the year before last. You know the police suspected me too. You can never really get out from underneath people's suspicions."

"Oh no, I'm so sorry, Claude. It's crazy how she disappeared, and all this time no one knows what happened."

Claude ate a piece of the banana nut muffin. He swallowed before speaking. "We argued the day before. I never imagined that I would never see her again. It's truly not a good idea to stay angry with someone."

Don't let the sun go down while you are still angry.

That's one of the few Bible verses I had learned over the years. I glanced over at Eleanor. I knew she'd finished writing a book a few months ago that was loosely based on Rebecca's disappearance. But I wasn't sure if Claude was aware of this.

"Well, maybe I can help." I shifted my weight from one foot to the other. "I've been thinking about what to investigate next for the *Cold Justice Podcast.* People keep asking me if I'm going to do a new season." I paused. "Do you think it would be a good idea for me to investigate Rebecca's disappearance?"

Claude furrowed his eyebrows. "Joss, I'm not sure if that's such a good idea. I mean, I appreciate the thought, but Rebecca's case... it's different."

I placed my hand on my hips. "Different how?"

He hesitated, looking down at his hands. "Rebecca was acting off in the weeks leading up to her disappearance. I don't want you getting involved in anything dangerous."

"Dangerous?" I commented. "What exactly was Rebecca involved in?"

Claude sighed, his shoulders slumping. "You mean who was she involved with? You would have to talk to these people to get a podcast going, and I'm not sure if that's a good idea." He suddenly sat up straighter. "Aren't you dating Detective Baez now?"

"Yes." I confessed with a blush.

Claude stated. "Maybe he can find out about where the investigation is right now. He might also have the same concerns as I do with you doing the podcast."

"Really? Claude, if there were people around Rebecca that could have caused her harm, why didn't the police approach them instead of bothering you?"

He shrugged. "I guess I was an easier target."

"Oh no."

Claude and I turned to Eleanor. She hadn't been contributing to the conversation, but her face appeared to be paler than usual as she looked over at Claude.

I asked. "What's wrong? Did you find something?"

Eleanor clasped her hands across her chest. "It's all over social media. They found the body of a woman."

I observed Claude. He gripped the table so hard his knuckles were white. With barely a whisper he asked, "Is it her?"

I wonder if that's where Andre was headed when he received the message on his phone earlier.

If this body really was Rebecca Montgomery, what happened to her? And why was she resurfacing now?

About the Author

Tyora Moody is the author of **Soul-Searching Mysteries,** which includes **cozy mystery, women sleuth mystery, and mystery romance** under the Christian Fiction genre. Her books include the Eugeena Patterson Mysteries, Joss Miller Mysteries, Serena Manchester Mysteries, Reed Family Mysteries, and the Victory Gospel Mysteries.

When Tyora isn't working for a literary client, she's either loving on her cats, listening to an audiobook or podcast, binge-watching crime shows or Marvel movies, and of course, thinking about the next book.

To contact Tyora about reviewing her books or book club discussions, visit her online at TyoraMoody.com.

Join her newsletter at https://tyoramoody.substack.com/

Tyora Moody's Books

Eugeena Patterson Mysteries

Deep Fried Trouble, #1

Oven Baked Secrets, #2

Lemon Filled Disaster, #3

A Simmering Dilemma, #4

An Unsavory Mess, #5

A Spicy Predicament, #6

Marinated Conditions, #7

Eugeena Patterson Family Shorts

Shattered Dreams, #1

A Blended Family Christmas, #2

Falling in Love... Again!, #3

Joss Miller Mysteries
Double Mocha Blues, #1
A Latte Mayhem, #2

Serena Manchester Mysteries
Hostile Eyewitness, prequel
Bittersweet Motives, #1
Dangerous Confessions, #2
Waning Innocence, #3
Presumed Guilty, #4

Reed Family Mysteries
Broken Heart, #1
Troubled Heart, #2
Relentless Heart, #3
With All My Heart, #3.5
Faithful Heart, #4
Wounded Heart, #5

Victory Gospel Series (Mysteries)
When Rain Falls, #1
When Memories Fade, #2
When Perfection Fails, #3

Victory Gospel Shorts (Sweet Romance)
The Replacement Date, #1
Southern Delights, #2

DOUBLE MOCHA BLUES

When Love Finds Me, #3
Nobody's Replacement, #4
A Southern Delights Christmas, #5
Holding on to Love, #6